TO THE BRINK

Matt Charles

Copyright © 2022 Matthew Stadnik

All rights reserved

The characters and events portrayed in this book are fictitious. Any similarity to real persons, living or dead, is coincidental and not intended by the author.

No part of this book may be reproduced, or stored in a retrieval system, or transmitted in any form or by any means, electronic, mechanical, photocopying, recording, or otherwise, without express written permission of the publisher.

Cover design by: Hamza Arif
Printed in the United States of America

*Dedicated to my mother and grandmother: my
number one fans and tireless editors.*

CONTENTS

Title Page
Copyright
Dedication
Part I   1
Chapter 1   2
Chapter 2   5
Chapter 3   11
Chapter 4   14
Chapter 5   27
Chapter 6   32
Chapter 7   35
Chapter 8   37
Chapter 9   39
Chapter 10   46
Chapter 11   54
Chapter 12   58
Chapter 13   61
Chapter 14   63
Chapter 15   65
Chapter 16   68
Chapter 17   70

Chapter 18	77
Part II	79
Chapter 19	80
Chapter 20	83
Chapter 21	85
Chapter 22	88
Chapter 23	91
Chapter 24	94
Chapter 25	97
Chapter 26	100
Chapter 27	101
Chapter 28	103
Chapter 29	105
Chapter 30	114
Chapter 31	117
Chapter 32	121
Chapter 33	134
Chapter 34	136
Part III	138
Chapter 35	139
Chapter 36	142
Chapter 37	148
Chapter 38	152
Chapter 39	154
Chapter 40	157
Chapter 41	159
Chapter 42	169
Chapter 43	179

Chapter 44	181
Chapter 45	187
Chapter 46	191
Chapter 47	208
Chapter 48	215
Chapter 49	218
Chapter 50	220
Chapter 51	222
Acknowledgement	229
About The Author	231

PART I

CHAPTER 1

Marquette, Michigan
November 1, 2027
1030 Hours EST

Mother Nature had undergone another mood swing, as she is so prone to do in the shoulder seasons across the Midwest. The streak of bleak, gloomy skies foretelling of the impending gales of November and subsequent deep freeze had been briefly traded in for sunshine and agreeable temperatures that called Rob Ranta outside for a hike. He was working his way up the steep rocky trails of Hogback Mountain, his mind drifting through a pensive reverie, the type of contemplation many denizens of the far north undergo as autumn beauty gives way to the unrelenting feral beast that is winter.

Michigan is certainly not known for large cliffs or mountains, however the sweeping geological feature known as the Canadian Shield carves down through the western half of the Upper Peninsula, adding rugged, stony features to the collection of swamps, meadows, and sand dunes that make up the rest of the state. As a consequence of the massive glacial movements of the Ice Age, the topsoil was scoured away leaving large swaths of exposed rock throughout the northern reaches of the Midwest and much of Canada. Hogback stood as one of the more dramatic monuments to this time, a sizable rocky mound rising over 500 feet up from the surrounding terrain, closely embraced by dense boreal forest up until the final knob where a bald, windswept peak provided humbling views of Lake Superior and the coastal region.

Despite the inviting combination of rejuvenating sunshine and a refreshingly cool breeze, Rob encountered few other souls on the trail. He scrambled his way up the final stony stretch to stand alone on the summit. He took in the panorama of brown, blue, and green, and the only sounds he heard were the slight whistle of wind gusts and the blood pounding in his head to the rhythm of his rapid heartbeat, hastened by the exertion of moving his one-hundred-and-eighty-pound body in opposition of gravity. As his pulse slowed, the grainy noise of the growing city drifted up to him, a reminder of the changes this land had undergone and was sure to continue to experience in the years to come.

The construction of the new rocket launch spaceport outside Marquette had just wrapped up one year prior, and the Superior Launch Site, or SLS, was drawing a considerable expansion to the small city. While Rob resided outside the city limits in the much smaller mining town of Ishpeming, he frequently visited Marquette both for business and pleasure. The population of the cozy municipality had grown by over 30% in the past few years, although Rob suspected this had as much to do with the changing climate as with the new spaceport. The unpredictable temperature swings and uncertain future of water access throughout large swaths of the Southwestern United States was driving an exodus towards the Great Lakes region. While this influx of desert dwellers primarily settled around the larger cities to the south like Chicago, Minneapolis, Milwaukee, and Detroit, a number of existing residents in those areas were flocking even farther north themselves, both to hedge against the creeping heat and drought, and to escape the crowding brought on by the newcomers.

Gazing out across the waters of mighty Lake Superior, Rob was struck by the scintillating dance of solar rays glinting off the emerald ripples on the surface of the monumental body of water. Though he had been around the immense lake his whole life, he still stood in wonder, appreciating the beauty and the value of this divine natural resource. His thoughts drifted to news of severe drought hitting large swaths of California, Nevada, and New Mexico. It felt strange knowing that millions of people at this very moment were experiencing strict water rationing and may eventually be forced to uproot and leave their homelands. Meanwhile he was surrounded by some of the largest deposits of freshwater on the planet.

Rob's meditation was disrupted by a low rumbling carrying over the trees through the crisp autumn air. By now he had become accustomed to the bass thundering that signaled a rocket launch, although the first time he was quite alarmed. Deep down in his evolutionary instinct, such forceful, visceral sounds were linked to danger or disaster on a titanic scale. As if nature hadn't delivered enough of a sensory treat already that day, now humanity would put on a display of its own.

He turned his gaze to the northwest and observed thick rolling clouds blossoming up from a spot on the coastline. A tall narrow object emerged from the smoke, rising inexorably towards the limits of the Earth's atmosphere. The rocket surged upward on wings of brilliant flame, the combustion of liquid oxygen and highly refined kerosene propelling it into the heavens, leaving a billowing streak of exhaust in its wake. Rob marveled at the projectile, a monument to human achievement. If we can harness chaos incarnate for our own grandiose designs, what aspects of the natural world would we not eventually master?

CHAPTER 2

13,000 feet over the Mojave Desert, California
November 1, 2029
1315 Hours PST

Maria Delgado soared across the skies in her Lockheed Martin F-22 Raptor, screaming through the clouds like a banshee of myth. Despite the various discomforts of the cockpit, she was in her element, where she felt she truly thrived. No earthbound venture quite matched the thrill of flying a fighter jet. There was certainly an air of magnificence to gaze down and see the ground from a god's eye view, but anyone could garner such an experience in a passenger plane. A select few, however, would ever know the heady exhilaration of blasting through the sound barrier or maneuvering at high speeds. An unnatural part of her relished the harsh pull of Gs on her body that left her on the edge of consciousness but made her feel most alive.

Maria "Slim" Delgado had become a full-fledged pilot for the United States Air Force just a few years prior. She may not have been top of her class, but she was still a highly capable pilot, and had demonstrated a near inhuman ability to withstand powerful G-forces. She was now stationed at Edwards Air Force Base as part of the 412th Test Wing. Her callsign lacked a comical or raunchy backstory, derived simply from a direct English translation of her last name. She was now almost an hour into a training exercise with the new Kratos XQ-58 Valkyrie "loyal wingman" drone craft. These Unmanned Combat Aerial Vehicles, or UCAVs, had been developed to serve as a lower cost force multiplier to the human controlled combat aircraft. They had a limited onboard artificial intelligence that allowed them to take basic combat actions against enemy forces, however for the most part they received commands directly from a controlling allied pilot. With nowhere near the speed and maneuvering capability of a true fighter jet, the drones could never match piloted fighters one for one on the battlefield, but working in conjunction with the manned craft they could vastly increase a pilot's threat profile.

The Valkyrie UCAVs were able to assist with electronic information warfare, absorb enemy missile fire, and carry missiles of their own. The latter item was, in Maria's opinion, the most valuable. Not only did this effectively give her a deep reserve of missiles to engage with, but each platform could also tag their own targets allowing her to deal with a number of enemies simultaneously. Each drone could be outfitted with up to eight missiles and flying with a pair of drones gave Maria quite the arsenal. One drawback was that the drones were not currently specced for supersonic flight, but she was sure the next generation would overcome that issue.

Today's little wargaming exercise pitted Maria and two of her colleagues in the nimble Raptor fighters, each commanding a complement of twin Valkyrie drones, against a squadron of six General Dynamics F-16 Fighting Falcons, all flown by other pilots within her group. This flight was part of an ongoing series of missions to help familiarize pilots with the drone wingman mechanics, as well as prove out the actual combat potential of the new unmanned craft.

Her squadron leader's voice came over the radio, "Echo One reading multiple bogies at heading zero-two-five degrees, how copy?"

Echo One, a pilot by the name of James "Joker" McCoy, had been one of her peers in the joint specialized undergraduate pilot training program. Maria had been paying close attention to her radar, and almost immediately after the transmission she saw a cluster of blips representing solid object detections off in the distance flash onto the display.

"Echo Two, good copy. I have them at four-three-zero miles," Maria responded. In this case when she said "miles" she really meant nautical miles. This was a farther detection than usual against the F-16s, the interlocking radar scans from the drones serving to boost the effective range at which her systems could coalesce radar returns into a confirmed physical object. The computers of each aircraft in her small unit, both human and AI operated, were all linked together to share radar detection data, allowing them to build on each other's individual pictures of the battle space and coordinate targeting.

"They probably don't see us yet. Let's adjust heading to minus zero-seven-zero degrees off present and kick it up to six hundred knots," James ordered.

"Echo Two copies."

"Echo Three, copy."

The two groups of aircraft were flying more or less head on, but Maria's group was now splitting off and taking a wide turn to come in from the "enemy's" side, which would give them less time to react once they spotted Maria and her wingmates.

A few minutes later James piped up again, "Count six bogies, all changing heading and coming around. Current approach closure rate seven-four-two knots. Let's lock 'em up and take 'em down."

Maria switched her radar targeting computer from search mode to track mode, zeroing in on one of the distant F-16s to lock on so her missile could track it. Though the Falcon jets were still over 200 nautical miles away, the AIM-260 Joint Advanced Tactical Missile, or JTAM, that Maria was prepping to "arm" could reach out and blast an enemy from the skies at ranges of up to 120 miles. This type of fighting, referred to as Beyond Visual Range or BVR, accounted for almost 100% of engagements these days. With the technology to strike with lethal accuracy from so far away, there was no reason to get into close range, or BFM, where Basic Fighter Maneuvers were employed in the style of classic dogfighting from the earlier world wars. Once a JTAM was fired, Maria's computer would continue to feed the missile information about the target to keep it on an intercept course. When the range closed, the missile would activate its own onboard active radar tracking and hound the target until it either brought down the quarry or ran out of fuel.

Since this was just a training run, Maria would go through the motions of locking on and initiating a missile launch but would not actually fire a missile at her compatriots in the OpFor fighters. A computer on the ground tracking all elements of the simulated combat would create a digital missile to match that of the one Maria "fired" and transmit its information profile to the computers of all the aircraft involved in the exercise. If the simulated missile made contact with a jet, that craft would be considered destroyed and the pilot would disengage from the operation.

Maria keyed into the drone command interface module to set her two Valkyries to Automatic Seek and Destroy mode. The drone AI algorithm would process targets, taking into account information from its own radar and that of its allies, and work out optimal firing solutions. In this mode, the drones would prioritize untargeted enemies first, ensuring each opponent had a missile sent their way, before stacking multiple missiles onto the same enemy.

"Fox three."

"Fox three!"

"Fox three."

The calls came over the lines from each pilot, announcing that they had just let loose an active radar guided missile. Her drone interface module confirmed that her Valkyries had fired missiles of their own and were tracking their progress. Moments later Maria heard a strident tone indicating that an enemy was tagging her with a missile lock of their own. The short beep was soon replaced by a continuous emission signaling an enemy radar lock.

"Vampires inbound."

"Going evasive."

Now that Maria's missile was on its way to her target,

she tugged on the flight controls and prepared to run maneuvers to dodge the hostile missile headed her way. She flipped her Valkyries into Adaptive Guardian mode, whereby their programmed routines would focus on evading enemy fire, and protecting her, their controller. Maria glanced at her flight computer which now highlighted the simulated incoming enemy missile. Three missiles, actually. As the distance between her and the missiles shrank, she began executing a series of sharp turns to throw the missiles off her path. With each turn she felt the strong pull of G-forces trying to drain the vital oxygen-delivering blood from her head, but she tensed up her muscles and fought back, maintaining her state of consciousness.

"Splash one bandit!" James hollered excitedly.

Maria noted an icon flash on her heads-up display indicating that her missile had not connected with its target.

"No joy on my end," she called out in between tight turns. Maria wanted to keep up the offensive in some way but still had to deal with playing defense against the supersonic warheads seeking to take her out of the fight. She punched in an order for one of her Valkyries to switch back to Seek and Destroy mode and fire until dry. The drone proceeded to lock up targets and send out digital JTAMs as quickly as it could achieve locks. Meanwhile, Maria saw that one of her pursuing missiles had fallen off her tail, but the other two were still coming in hot. She keyed in a chaff dump, hoping to fool the other missiles with the bogus radar signature. It worked on one, leaving one remaining. Her mind raced, trying to come up with a way out, knowing she only had moments until "impact." Right then, the other Valkyrie in guardian mode, which had been mirroring her movements almost perfectly, went into a long roll sideways and intercepted the missile.

The status icon of the Valkyrie drone on her display went dark, signifying that it was now removed from the fight. Maria steadied her breathing and returned her attention to the dogfight. Her second drone had loosed seven missiles before being taken out by a missile itself. Echo three and his drones were down for the count as well, but James and one of his Valkyries were still standing. Four of the F-16s had disappeared from her display, and the other three were in the midst of wild evasive maneuvers, clearly dealing with some of the remaining missiles from her side.

James came in over her headset, "Let's press the advantage and wrap up this rodeo, Slim."

"Affirmative, Joker." Normally the pilots would stick to tactical callouts during a mission and not resort to the informal callsigns. James's callsign of "Joker" had been earned partially from his lack of comms discipline, though. Feeling elated by the way the mock battle was unfolding, Maria joined in his little breach of protocol.

James and Maria throttled up towards the last of the opposing Falcons and delivered a coup de grâce in the form of a pair of AIM-9X Sidewinder infrared seeking air-to-air missiles.

"Fox two!"

"Fox two."

The distracted F-16 pilots were in no position to avoid the tenacious tracking of the sidewinders and James and Maria each chalked up another "kill" to close out the exercise.

"Sierra Hotel, kiddos," the voice of Echo Three sounded in their ears. "Looks like drinks are on me tonight."

CHAPTER 3

Ishpeming, Michigan
March 1, 2030
0700 Hours EST

Rob lay in bed, running his thumb over the crystalline aluminum oxide screen of his smartphone. His feet hadn't even touched the floor yet and he was already absorbing news stories from events occurring across the globe, and even some far above the planet's surface in outer space. These days, "water" was the pervasive buzzword, specifically referencing the lack of water plaguing many areas of the United States. His country had managed to survive the rabidly tumultuous political division of the '20s, only to be gripped by a crisis of environmental maladaptation. Large population centers across the West and Southwestern regions of the country appeared to be on the verge of collapse, at least so the reports claimed, and food production was suffering as large swathes of farmland were left parched and infertile.

Gazing out his rectangular bedroom window at the two feet of grainy, glistening snowpack blanketing his lawn and frosting the dormant trees, it was difficult to envision the scenario facing his fellow countrymen. One headline, however, did bring the situation home to a reality he could more readily identify with. Construction of the transcontinental Lake Superior pipeline was slated to commence in June. The project would put into practice a scheme that had been floating around for as long as the union had held the forty-eight contiguous states: pumping freshwater from the deep reserves of the Great

Lakes and distributing it to drier areas of the country in need.

At a glance, the idea of taking water from the great lakes and spreading it around appeared entirely reasonable. The quadrillions of gallons of water held in the mighty inland oceans was well beyond what the entire population that had cropped up along the expansive shores of the famed lakes needed to sustain themselves. Why not share the wealth? For a short time, such a transaction would indeed work. The power put into ramping the water up over the continental divide could be reclaimed on the other end as the water rushed back down to lower elevations, neatly solving for that issue as well.

The inconvenient snag in the equation was the fact that every gallon of water removed from the Great Lakes watershed was a gallon that would not easily return. All that water pumped outside the watershed would not be replaced, and the water levels in the lake would soon begin to fall. The voluminous lakes could certainly support a regional population well in excess of the current level, but they could not sustainably provide for those living far outside the geographic locality.

This was clearly evidenced by the system that had already been established outside of Chicago, draining water from Lake Michigan for use across Southern California. While establishment of the colossal pumping operation had been vehemently opposed by members of the Great Lakes Compact, the state of Illinois had blessed the proposal. The federal government sat on its hands, and without any higher legal authority to intervene, construction moved forward.

A dubious deal had been reached whereby California would reverse the flow and return the "borrowed" water once the expansive desalination infrastructure being built all along the western coast became fully active. Progression of the highly energy intensive desalination plants had been inexplicably blocked and railroaded time and again within the California legislative system, and as a result the timeline of seeing meaningful returns was significantly delayed. Nevertheless, enough sentiment had built up within the Chicago area to send off the life-giving water to those without, and the public seemed to more or less embrace the entire proposition.

Only two years later, the water level of Lake Michigan had dropped over six feet, and dissension was rising. Groups had rallied from around the area pushing to turn off the pump, but the Illinois legislature, with assurances, and undoubtedly some under the table kickbacks, from California, stood firm. On top of that, the nonstop flow traveling thousands of miles across the country wasn't enough to remedy the problem out west. Now, the same group of parochial aristocrats had their sights set on drawing from Lake Superior as well. Once again, they faced stiff opposition.

Efforts to place a pump near Duluth had stalled out as nobody would give up the land rights needed to construct a site on the coast. Instead, the wealthy moguls angling to set up the pump brokered a deal with the exclusive and insular Huron Mountain Club to set up on their land. The Huron Mountain Club had been established over a century ago and now held over 20,000 acres of land in the central Upper Peninsula of Michigan, including miles of Lake Superior shoreline. Membership in the club was reserved for a select few with the right connections and affluence to match. The land served as a getaway and a sportsman's paradise for the handful of magnates lucky enough to obtain membership, and access was highly restricted. Now that privacy would be used to make an uninterrupted grab for the bounty of the Big Lake.

Rob rolled over and slid his legs off the mattress, resting his phone on the nightstand and readying himself for the day ahead. As he worked through the motions of his morning routine, the story about the Lake Superior pump kept niggling at him. The idea of violating the sanctity of the great lake he had grown up around was anathema to him. He struggled to come to grips with the notion that a small cabal of greedy, shortsighted elites could orchestrate such an atrocity, counter to the will of millions of people surrounding the area. Someone had to take action against this.

CHAPTER 4

Luzon, Philippines
March 3, 2030
0200 Hours PHT

Kenneth Hyde contemplated the mission ahead as he sat crammed in the tight confines of a Shallow Water Combat Submersible with his five teammates, cruising beneath the murky midnight waves of the Pacific Ocean off the coast of the Philippine island of Luzon. The 30-year-old SEAL from Nebraska and his DEVGRU SEAL team had been tasked with rescuing a high value CIA intelligence asset being held at a Chinese black site situated along the rocky coastline.

The operation seemed straightforward on paper: approach the compound from the water, locate and secure the VIP, deal with a small handful of guards in the process, then catch a quick ride out via helicopter. Easy day. If there was one lesson Kenneth had learned in his years of service, it was that no mission ever went as planned. As far as weapons-free ops went though, this ranked low on the Charlie Foxtrot potential scale.

"Thirty seconds out, prep for debark," Kenneth's team leader, Baxter, stated in a low, calm voice.

Kenneth checked his equipment over for what must have been at least the tenth time. He was wearing full diving gear over a tight-fitting black wetsuit. Slung around his neck was a compact SIG MCX Rattler with an integrated suppressor and an advanced Vortex Fire Control System optic mounted on top. At his feet was a bulky watertight duffel with the rest of his kit that he would swap to once on land.

"Beginning cabin flood," Baxter announced, and water began trickling into the passenger compartment of the small submersible. The inside chamber would fill with water, matching the outside pressure, at which point the side hatches would open allowing the SEAL team to swim the remaining distance to their beachhead.

Kenneth began taking breaths through his SCUBA regulator as the tepid water enveloped him. Seconds later the hatch slid back, and he elegantly slipped out of the submersible along with the lithe dark forms of his teammates and began propelling himself towards the shore with his long composite rubber flippers. Kenneth pierced through the pleasantly warm embrace of the dark waters and his feet soon found purchase on the pebbly ocean bed as he prepared to breach the surface.

The SEAL team members slowly materialized from the placid ocean, appearing like fearsome Lovecraftian sea-dwellers come to drag hapless human souls back down to the depths below. They crept through thigh-deep water towards the thin sandy beach that abutted a short craggy cliff line, then formed up among a cluster of angular boulders at the base of the cliff. The amphibious operators took turns covering each other with short-barreled Rattler rifles scanning up and down the narrow coast, while they cracked open waterproof gear-bags and swapped kits in pairs. Kenneth traded his slim SCUBA tank, breathing system, facemask, and swim fins for a ballistic helmet with an integrated radio communication system and optoelectronics, and a vest loaded with ceramic armor plates, extra magazines, and other critical combat components.

Once the transition was complete, they hooked the shucked-off diving gear to a tether leading back to the submersible, then Baxter sent a command through his sleek wrist computer for the small watercraft to autonomously return to the Virginia-class nuclear submarine from which it had initially been launched. Kenneth took in his surroundings. A sliver of moonlight, unobstructed by any cloud cover, illuminated the coastline just enough for his well-adjusted eyes to see without the assistance of his night observation device. The night air had lost most of the tropical heat of the daytime, but retained the moisture, creating a thick blanket of humidity. Beads of sweat were already replacing the drops of salty ocean water languidly evaporating off patches of exposed skin. Nestled against the steep, rocky coast, the compound they were hitting was located in a very tactically sound position that should have been impervious to an approach from the sea. Such an assessment failed to account for Navy SEALs.

One member of the team, Jackson, had yet to put on his armored vest. Instead, he was scouting along the vertical rock face for the best path upwards. Once he had a line located, he secured a climbing rope to a hardpoint on the harness around his waist and began to work his way up the cliff. Loaded down with just the weight of his sidearm and a few pieces of climbing gear dangling from the harness, Jackson fingered small crimps and cracks in the rock to pull his body up the thirty-foot wall of stone. Once at the top, he set up an anchor for the rope he had dragged up with him, allowing his teammates to follow him up the cliff using the rope to assist their climb.

At the top of the cliff, Baxter checked in with the other elements of the operation, including a drone operator and helicopter crew aboard a Zumwalt-class destroyer miles off the coast, and CIA analysts halfway around the world in Langley, Virginia.

"Romeo One for Home Plate," Baxter transmitted.

"Go for Home Plate," came a disembodied response.

"We're in position at the rear of the compound. How are we looking?"

"Copy Romeo, we have you on the scope. We're tagging two Tangos for you we picked up on thermals. We estimate another four to six bodies inside. You have the green light to make entry."

The drone operator keeping constant high-altitude surveillance on the area had the ability to "tag" targets for the SEAL team. Any positively identified enemy combatants would be marked with a red diamond that would show up within the field of view of the FCS optics mounted on each of the SEALs' rifles, highlighting hostiles that the commandos may not have been able to visually acquire themselves. While Kenneth would never fully rely on a drone over his own two eyes to identify where enemy shooters were or were not, it was certainly helpful to have as much information as possible when assaulting an occupied structure.

The SEAL team split into two groups of three to enter the compound. Rifle raised, Kenneth cautiously stepped along the outside wall towards a doorway, where he and his two teammates stacked up for entry. Kenneth lightly tested the doorknob, finding it locked. He then called up one of his men, Pochenko, to address the lock. Pochenko held a thermite breaching pen to the lock while Kenneth and the third man, Doyle, stood on either side of him with rifles aimed at the door.

"Romeo Four, breaching," Pochenko whispered into his throat mic, broadcasting to the rest of the operational personnel.

The SEAL ignited the breaching pen, and a thin gout of flame burning at over 5,000 degrees Fahrenheit melted through the locking mechanism. Kenneth and Doyle swiftly glided through the doorway, splitting the room in half and clearing each corner with the muzzles of their rifles. Encountering nobody in the small mudroom, the trio crept down a corridor towards another wider room, where a single red diamond marked the presence of at least one armed and dangerous individual.

A light fixture in the next room was casting a muted orange glow out across the corridor, and Kenneth stood at the light's edge, waiting for the affirming grip of Pochenko's hand on his shoulder to indicate that his comrades were ready to move. Upon receiving the signal, Kenneth wheeled around the corner with his weapon up, scanning for threats in the far left third of the space.

Precisely where the hovering red diamond projected onto

the holographic film of his weapon's optic indicated stood a man with Asiatic features staring out a window, one hand wrapped around the grip of an Uzi submachine gun, the other pinching a smoldering cigarette. Kenneth allowed the crosshair of his optic to float across the side of the man's face, coming to rest next to the man's ear. Then he squeezed the trigger.

The firing pin of his rifle made contact with the primer of the chambered cartridge, igniting the propellant and causing a rapid expansion of gasses to expel the copper-jacketed lead projectile on a path towards the head of the unaware compound guard. Kenneth's MCX rifle was loaded with .300 AAC Blackout ammunition which would fire bullets at a velocity slower than the speed of sound so as not to emit the loud crack that a supersonic bullet would make as it pierced the sound barrier. Combined with the rifle's suppressor, Kenneth's shot was whisper quiet.

The subsonic bullet impacted the man's skull right between his ear and his eye, piercing the cranial bone and tearing through brain matter. The bullet's destructive path through the brain disrupted the neural activity of electric signals passing commands through the nervous system, causing the man's body to drop limply to the floor. Kenneth tracked the body on its way down through his optic and sent one more round into the skull of the lifeless corpse, causing it to twitch with the impact.

"E.K.I.A." Kenneth vocalized into his throat mic, letting his team know that he had taken down one enemy.

The rest of the room was clear, and the three operators proceeded down a stairway into a basement level. The stairs led into a dingy cellar with earthen walls. Within the tight quarters of the cellar, lit by a single lightbulb hanging tenuously from the ceiling, a man with a QSZ-92 9mm pistol holstered at his side straddled a wooden chair, watching over the supine form of another individual on the floor whose hands were bound behind his back. After taking in the scene, Kenneth's rifle coughed twice, liberating two more bullets from their shell casings and planting them into the back of the seated man's head. Pochenko slung his rifle and rushed forward to the prone figure, pulling his face up into the light and comparing what he saw to an image of the individual they were seeking to rescue that had been downloaded to his wrist computer.

"Positive ID on the asset, repeat, positive ID on the asset," Pochenko called into his mic.

"Copy that," Baxter responded, "The rest of the building is clear. We have three hostile KIAs. Regroup in the main hallway and let's move to exfil."

Then Baxter addressed the helicopter crew that was on standby in a holding pattern over the ocean, well outside visual range of the island. "Big Bird this is Romeo One. We are ready for exfil. Moving to the LZ now."

"Copy Romeo One. Big Bird is en route. ETA twelve Mikes."

Pochenko had drawn a small folding knife and freed the captive CIA asset from binding restraints. Kenneth walked up and addressed the man, who had a weary, vacant look in his dark baggy eyes.

"We're with the U.S. Navy, and we're here to bring you home. Follow me and we'll get the hell out of here."

The man stared for a second, registering his change of fortune, then croaked out a dry, raspy "okay."

The six-man SEAL team and their one rescued prisoner filed through the compound and out towards a wide driveway designated as the helicopter landing zone. Suddenly a voice cut in over the radio.

"Romeo this is Home Plate. Be advised we're tracking a convoy of four vehicles heading through the village in your direction. Unclear what their intentions are but they are assumed to be hostile."

"Copy Home Plate. Keep us updated on their path," Baxter replied.

The rest of Romeo team had already taken up positions behind a low stone wall running along the driveway or pillars lining the courtyard of the compound.

"Convoy is turning onto your street. We're also seeing two more large vans moving through the village farther out," a drone operator announced.

"Romeo team, prepare for imminent contact," Baxter called into his headset, "Big Bird, what's your ETA?"

"Big Bird is still ten Mikes out, making best speed."

"Alright, we're looking at a hot LZ so let's make this quick."

"Acknowledged, Romeo. LZ is hot."

The Special Operations Aviation Regiment pilot's voice was calm and flat, completely unperturbed. *This guy was one cool customer*, thought Kenneth. Based on his experience, he imagined these pilots would fly through an active volcano without blinking an eye. Hell, if they were operating in the South Pacific they probably had flown through a volcano at some point and come out the other end unphased.

The first car in the convoy, a modern looking jeep, skidded to a halt fifty yards from the compound, soon joined by the other three vehicles. Dark figures began jumping out from open doors and making towards the compound. Kenneth could discern the shapes of firearms in the hands of the approaching figures. He and his SEAL brothers didn't wait for any other signal. As one they opened up with their SIG rifles, sending a silent storm of lead towards the group of armed belligerents.

Eight men dropped to the ground from the opening barrage, and the rest immediately began scampering for cover and firing blindly towards the compound. Kenneth could make out the staccato sounds of Chinese Type 95 rifles, peppering the area around him and his team with $5.8 \times 42mm$ rounds. The CIA asset was in a low crouch next to Kenneth, behind a stucco wall. Kenneth pressed the man flat onto the dirt and in a sharp low voice told him "Don't move. Stay down there."

Red diamonds quickly began to appear in his weapon's optic as the drone operator started tagging targets. In the low light, with silenced weapons and massive technological superiority, the SEALs were able to keep the attackers at bay. But with two-to-one odds still favoring the assaulting force, the sheer volume of firepower was preventing the SEAL team from quickly ending the fight. Kenneth peaked out and drew a bead on a man dressed in civilian clothes and unleashing fully automatic fire towards his location. Kenneth squeezed off a tight burst of quiet gunfire and the man spun over backwards. Another hostile made a wide run for a flank attempt but was mercilessly cut down by a member of the SEAL team.

Kenneth heard a loud grunt as a 5.8mm bullet met the flesh of one of his teammates, but all six men kept on returning fire. All at once the red diamonds winked out, then the frantic voice of the drone operator came through his headset.

"Romeo, Romeo, do you read? I've just lost all signal from the drone. I think we're being jammed."

"Romeo-" a slight pause followed by muffled gunshots "- reads loud and clear. We can still hear you," Baxter responded.

"OK Romeo, those vans should be pulling up any second now. You're on your own though," the drone operator warned.

"Big Bird?" Baxter inquired into the radio.

"Seven Mikes."

"Copy."

No complaints. Just a simple acknowledgement of the circumstance as they stood.

When the two vans pulled up, the tempo of the battle instantly changed. Black clad heavily armored figures disembarked and began sending a hail of disciplined fire towards the SEAL positions.

"Aw shit," muttered Jackson. "I think these guys are Sea Dragons."

The "Sea Dragons," more formally known as the Jiaolong Commandos, were an elite group of Chinese operators. Trained in all types of warfare but with an emphasis on maritime operations, the Sea Dragons were in some ways equivalent to the U.S. Navy SEALs. Kenneth leaned out to fire another burst but had to quickly duck back behind cover as bullets chewed into the dirt and stone around him. A series of explosive pops sounded as the Chinese commandos sent a volley of 20mm airburst grenades over the stone walls of the compound.

"Doyle is down!" Pochenko shouted over the comm. Doyle may not be dead, but he was no longer combat effective. One less gun in a battle where every gun was crucial.

Kenneth dropped low and angled his rifle around the corner, knocking a Chinese operator to the ground with three rapid hits. As he rolled back behind the wall, white-hot pain lanced through his right shoulder. He knew he'd been shot, but he was still in the fight, so he put the thought aside and continued to engage the enemy, adjusting his firing posture to accommodate his new injury.

A cry of "Last mag!" came from someone in the squad. Kenneth was almost out of rifle ammunition himself, having only brought four magazines, giving him a total of one hundred and twenty shots.

"Romeo Two, applying tourniquet, down for thirty," the SEAL named Ramirez called out, letting the team know that we would be briefly out of action while he tended to a serious wound.

The newly arrived Chinese force must have had a drone of their own that they were using to identify the SEALs' positions, in addition to canceling out the SEALs' own previous informational advantage.

Kenneth saw Jackson hit the deck after letting off a sustained salvo, bullets kicking up dust and vaporized stone from the crest of the low wall he had flattened himself behind. As Jackson flopped down, an empty magazine fell with him, and he had a fresh one slammed in as soon as he was on the ground. As enemy fire shifted towards Jackson's hide, Pochenko leaned out around a corner and squeezed off a chain of semi-automatic rifle shots before running dry, at which point he seamlessly dropped his rifle to hang on the sling around his neck and in the same motion drew his Glock 19 sidearm and continued engaging with 9mm pistol rounds. The volume of hostile fire notably picked up and Baxter yelled to the team.

"Five of 'em pushing up the driveway, at you Jackson!"

The situation had gone from very bad to even worse, and the enemy must have been gaining confidence, recognizing that they now had massive fire superiority over their opposition. By rights the battle should have ended minutes ago. Mathematically the six SEALs simply stood no chance against a platoon of more than sixteen well trained and better equipped Chinese special forces operators augmented by the twenty or so irregulars, most likely local thugs with guns. At this point every member of the SEAL team had sustained at least one significant injury, and one of them was out of the fight altogether. Any rational human being who valued their life would throw down their weapon and wave the white flag in this situation. *There was one variable throwing off that math though*, Kenneth thought to himself.

SEALs never quit.

Kenneth was forced to crawl along his wall to reposition as bullets poured into the area he had been firing from moments ago, his shoulder screaming with pain the whole way. He couldn't get a good picture of the enemy's advance, but he saw Ramirez hobble out from behind a pillar and dump an entire magazine down the driveway before a round caught him center mass. His ceramic armor plate must have taken the impact since Kenneth watched Ramirez prop himself back up behind the pillar and reload. Through the chaos of battle and chorus of rifle fire, Kenneth imagined he heard the low rhythmic beating of helicopter blades.

Kenneth had now rotated to a new spot along the compound wall. He glanced back to make sure the CIA asset was still safely behind cover, then popped out to fend off the assault on Jackson's position. Jackson was lying prone ten feet from the corner of the low driveway wall with his weapon aimed high. Kenneth saw a black armored soldier rush around the corner towards Jackson, holding his rifle out and firing blindly at where he thought the SEAL positioned there might be. The soldier was immediately blown off his feet by a close-range burst of .300 Blackout rounds to the torso and head. Kenneth fired multiple rapid bursts from his own rifle at a pair of operators following behind the first soldier. The second man went down hard, but the third dove back and to the side, taking shelter on the opposite side of the wall from Jackson. Jackson, in a demonstration of preternatural situation awareness, hopped to his feet and whipped his rifle over the top of the low wall, emptying a savage volley into the covering commando on the other side.

Meanwhile the thumping of rotor blades, which turned out to be real after all, had grown louder.

"Big Bird is on site and putting down now, load up in twenty seconds," came the even-keeled voice of the helicopter pilot.

Kenneth glanced upwards and saw a Sikorsky HH-60 Pave Hawk sliding through the sky towards the clearing of the driveway. A brief high-pitched whine heralded a coming storm of violence as the door gunner spun up the barrels of an M134 Minigun. Without further preamble, the gunner cut loose with a buzzing stream of lead. The six barrels of the Minigun were cycling at their maximum rate, spitting out one hundred 7.62x51mm rounds per second. Bullets sparked off the metal body of the helicopter as Chinese commandos adjusted their fire to meet the new threat, but the chopper gunner methodically worked the rotary machine gun across the battlefield, silencing any return fire. The mighty weapon tore through vehicles like a firehose going through paper, eviscerating bodies caught in the path, both armored and unarmored.

"Go, go, go, get aboard now!" Baxter shouted, straining to be heard over the beating of the helicopter.

Kenneth sprinted over to the CIA asset, scooped him up, and hauled him bodily over to the helicopter bay door. The door gunner continued to fire while the SEALs limped aboard, dragging their wounded with them. A cascade of spent shell casings poured down around the men as they climbed up into the passenger bay. After six men had boarded, Baxter jumped up into the chopper himself, screaming at the pilot as he entered.

"We're all aboard, take off take off!"

The helicopter leapt up into the sky, then banked sharply and took off low across the ocean. As the aircraft peeled away from the haze of the coastal battleground, the gunner finally let up. Only, Kenneth noted, because his one-hundred-pound ammunition hopper had run dry. Wispy smoke oozed from the glowing barrels, which must have been on the verge of warping from overheating. The gunner turned towards the SEALs arranged in the passenger bay, his features strained tight with tension and focus. Then a wide grin cracked across his face.

"WOOO, get some!" he shouted with unbridled enthusiasm, one fist pumping the air next to his head. The surging adrenaline of surviving an intense two-way gunbattle, coupled with the primal satisfaction of sending two thousand rounds downrange had him giddy with nervous excitement.

"Hell yeah, brother," Jackson chanted, extending his arm straight out towards the gunner and making a fist with his hand, which was promptly met with the knuckles of the gunner's own fist.

Baxter and Pochenko had stabilized Doyle, whose face, arms, and legs were pocketed with bloody shrapnel wounds, and were now tending to the gunshot wound on Ramirez's thigh. Kenneth had applied a hemostatic dressing to his shoulder, which the bullet appeared to have passed through cleanly. He turned to the CIA asset they had extracted from the compound.

"So, spook. What intel do you have up in that head of yours that's so vital to Uncle Sam?"

The CIA operative stared solemnly at him for a second before replying.

"Sorry, I can't disc-"

"Oh, cut the bullshit," Kenneth interrupted, "We all nearly bought it pulling your ass out of that little hellhole. Least you can do is share with us what little tidbit of gossip we went to all that trouble for."

The CIA man considered this for a few moments then shrugged and began telling Kenneth what he had found out.

MATT CHARLES

What Kenneth heard made his blood run ice cold in his veins.

CHAPTER 5

Powell, Michigan
June 15, 2030
0805 Hours EST

Spring arrived with a flourish in the Upper Peninsula. The melting snow flooded the lowland regions, turning dusty dirt roads to muddy mires and unleashing swarms of mosquitoes and black flies across the wetlands and low-lying forests. After a good week of warm temperatures and sunshine, the network of forest roads had reformed into a usable condition, but the insects had only increased in number. All that mattered to the construction firms though, was that they could move heavy machinery across the unpaved roads.

Rob bounced around in the passenger seat of an old Ford Raptor pickup truck being driven by his older brother, Jason. They were on their way up to one such forest road that served as the only point of entry for accessing the small cove situated within the Huron Mountain Club's territory along the southern shore of Lake Superior where construction of the Superior Pipeline was slated to begin today. The two brothers were meeting up with a band of concerned locals and other activists who were planning to protest the pipeline and intended to block the path so that construction could not begin. Not a single construction outfit in the region had made a bid for the project, so a company from a few states over had been brought in to take on the work.

Jason was seven years older than Rob. Their father had served in the United States Army as part of the 101st Airborne

Division, completing two tours of duty in Afghanistan in the mid-2000s. Jason was dead set on following in his father's footsteps and enlisting as soon as he turned 18; however, that plan fell apart when their father returned for a third tour in the Middle East and was killed in action. Jason knew that without their father in the picture, it would fall on him to serve as Rob's role model through the crucial years of Rob's adolescence. So it was that Jason took on local employment in the mining industry, digging deep into the hard crust of the earth to excavate veins of iron ore from the extensive Negaunee Iron Formation. Naturally, Rob had followed Jason into that industry when he was of age.

Rob glanced over at his older brother, the man who had been a father and mentor to him throughout his middle school and high school years.

"So, you think we can actually stop 'em?" Rob queried. "Like, we just sit there in the way, and they'll give up and go home?"

"I'm not sure how it will play out. Alls I know is they ain't desecrating our lake." Jason replied.

The truck pulled up to a milling crowd right outside the border of the Huron Mountain Club's property line. About fifty or so people were gathered, with a pair of large lifted pickup trucks positioned in a makeshift roadblock, impeding the path of any vehicles attempting to continue down the road. Some protesters had signs, others held firearms, as had become the norm over the past decade for protests in a country where the second amendment to the nation's constitution still granted all citizens the inviolate right to bear arms.

The brothers hopped out of their vehicle, parked in a jumble of other cars and trucks along the grassy shoulder of the road, and slipped into the crowd. Jason found one of his acquaintances from work and began conversing, about what Rob could not discern over the chattering voices of the assembly. After twenty minutes of standing around swatting flies and shading his eyes from the climbing mid-morning sun, a message burbled through the crowd: "They're coming."

A few minutes later, Rob heard the rumble of heavy trucks and construction vehicles making their way down the sandy dirt road. The lead truck eased to a stop after rounding a bend and seeing the blockade before it. Shouts and jeers rose from the protesters, lambasting the construction crew with calls to turn around and go home. The sun rose in the sky while the construction convoy sat idle. The black flies were out in force, but the size of the crowd provided such a target rich environment that no single person was made to suffer the full wrath of the swarm. Eventually one individual, who Rob surmised was the foreman, stepped out from a truck and began speaking with some of the protesters at the head of the mass. Rob couldn't make out any words, but the foreman's expression remained sour throughout.

Additional vehicles carrying protesters continued trickling in, lining the sides of the road. About an hour had passed since the arrival of the construction vehicles when a black truck with the words "Marquette County Sheriff" emblazoned in curving gold lettering on the sides joined the stack of cars. Out stepped a tall, thick figure wearing a wide brimmed Stetson hat, dark brown shirt with a six-pointed star pinned over his heart, sharply creased khaki pants, and highly polished leather boots. A packed utility belt surrounded his waist and holstered at his side was a shoebox-sized silver Smith and Wesson .500 revolver.

The Sheriff strolled down the line of construction vehicles to the center of the gathering where the leaders of the protesters were staring down the construction foreman. Rob had weaved himself through the throng of people and was now within earshot of the ensuing exchange.

"Gentlemen," the Sheriff began, *"Ladies,"* he inflected, briefly tipping his hat towards a group of female protesters, "What, precisely, is going on here?"

Raised voices from both sides tried shouting over each other until the Sheriff raised his hand. Pointing to the foreman, he said "You first."

"Well, it's quite simple. We have a job to do down the road here, and these hooligans are obstructing us," the foreman stated, placing a disdainful emphasis on the word "hooligans."

"And what is this job you have to do?" Inquired the sheriff.

"We're building a pumping station on the shoreline, in the little bay up there," the foreman answered, gesticulating in the direction they were headed.

"That so? You wouldn't happen to have any documentation from the Great Lakes Compact council granting approval for this project, would you?"

"Look, I'm not the one pulling strings behind all this. I just build what I'm told to build, where I'm told to build it. Now this is a public road, and these people are illegally blocking it. Why don't you enforce some law and order right here and get them to clear out?"

"Sir, these people are exercising their protected right to protest actions which they deem as unjust. Meanwhile, it seems to me that *you* have no legal standing to be undertaking this construction project of yours. I think you better turn your boys around and leave my county. Better yet, leave my state."

The foreman stared blankly while expressions of shock and rage took turns twitching across his face. After collecting himself, he forced an air of calm and responded.

"Officer, may I ask for your name and badge number?"

"I'm Sheriff Keith Halper, badge is right here" he said, tapping his badge.

The foreman pulled out his smartphone and took a picture of Halper's badge.

"Alright, *Sheriff*, we'll do as you say. But I'm warning you, this project goes up a lot higher than you and your little podunk backwoods jurisdiction. Our job's going to get done one way or another, and I think you would be well advised to keep out of the way."

"Duly noted. Now you have a nice day, sir."

With that, the hulking construction vehicles began

ponderously reversing and turning around, heading back in the direction of the city.

CHAPTER 6

Castaic Lake Recreation Area, California
June 15, 2030
0900 Hours PST

The unrelenting southern California sun was still working its way up to the optimal angle from which to bake the arid desert earth as Maria and James briskly ascended the dusty rock-strewn trail through the crinkly sprawl of mountains guarding what remained of Castaic Lake. The pair wordlessly plowed through the steep, desolate terrain, both focusing on reaching the unnamed peak looming ahead of them before an hour elapsed on the stopwatch which had been started as soon as they exited their car on the side of a rugged fire road nearly four miles and a couple thousand vertical feet away.

While it was great to get off the military airbase for a bit of real-world recreation, the two dedicated pilots couldn't help but work a bit of physical training into their down time. Despite what the average infantryman might believe, piloting a fighter jet was very physically demanding, and being test pilots in the vaunted 412th, they held themselves to an even higher standard. That wasn't to say that Maria wasn't thoroughly enjoying the aggressive morning hike, dripping in sweat and sucking in ragged breaths though she was. Her unit had been especially busy recently running a battery of tests on the new F-25 Storm Crow stealth tactical fighter aircraft, which had won the bid to replace the F-22 Raptor as the next generation of air superiority fighter for the United States Air Force, giving her all the more reason to cherish the time off.

The early morning sun bathing the endless ranges of hills and mountains created a panorama of serene beauty. Stout, ornery bushes and scrub trees dotted the landscape, offering some proof of life in the scene. Maria wasn't able to truly appreciate her surroundings until she crested the exposed mountain top and finally stopped for a break. A glance at her watch told her she had been moving for fifty-seven minutes. Not bad.

After another minute of silence while she and James both got their breathing under control, Maria began to verbalize the thoughts that had been manifesting in her mind during the intense aerobic bout.

"You can barely see the lake now..."

"Yeah, I know," replied James, "It's, well, it's alarming really."

Maria had been referring to the distant Castaic Lake, one of the largest reservoirs in the Southwest supplying a sizable chunk of water and electricity to the region. Following a pattern seen with many reservoirs in the area, the water level had been steadily dropping over the previous years. Increased drought levels coupled with an ever-expanding demand as the population depending on the local resources grew was taking its toll.

"The beaches and rec area below the dam are still closed. At this rate it doesn't look like they'll open it up at all," James observed. "Can't spare anything to fill the lagoon just so people can have fun I suppose."

Maria didn't respond, taking in both the view and the implication of the exchange.

"Get this," James began conspiratorially, "a buddy of mine in the Air Guard mentioned his unit is being mobilized for some potential action. I mean something stateside. He says command won't go into details, but rumor is they're on alert in case things go poorly with the pipeline."

Maria, along with just about every other resident of Southern California, was very familiar with "the pipeline." She had mixed feelings about it. On the one hand, a reliable source of freshwater was desperately needed, but it seemed odd to her that they would draw water from thousands of miles away when they had vast oceans right next door. Of course, the salt-infused water wouldn't be much use for drinking, but that could be overcome. It baffled Maria that the desalination plants were still not active yet when the technology had been available for years.

"So, what, they'll go and bomb the Midwest if they don't give us their water?" Maria proposed with an air of cynical mirth.

"I don't know. I can't imagine that being the case but is anything ever totally off the table these days?"

"We should be saving our war-making energy for the real threats, like China and Russia," Maria opined.

"You're preaching to the choir. Whichever way things go, the future promises to be…interesting at least," James offered.

"Sure, I guess that's one way to see it…" Maria responded. "Anyway, let's start heading down. I can feel it's gonna be another hot one."

With that, the pair began jogging down the faint trail back towards the car.

CHAPTER 7

Negaunee, Michigan
June 20, 2030
2200 Hours EST

Rob and Jason sat side by side on worn leather barstools, each slowly sipping on a local brew in Barr's Bar, one of the long-standing family-owned taverns in downtown Negaunee. "Downtown" being used quite generously to describe a quarter of a square mile containing a collection of shops, restaurants, and other township essentials. There wasn't much of a crowd, just a few other miners and a couple summer tourists. The wistful voice of Gordon Lightfoot floated out from a pair of speakers making up a modernized jukebox in one corner. On some nights, patrons could even enjoy live music in the intimate confines of the establishment. The dim interior matched the sky outside where the high-latitude summer sun was just now fading over the horizon.

"Anything new on the pipeline?" Rob asked.

Rob knew that a group of volunteers were camped out at the makeshift roadblock, taking rotations to monitor the area around the clock to ensure none of the construction contractors slipped through with their heavy machinery to get to work. Aside from that knowledge and a few opaque news stories, it wasn't clear to him exactly what direction things were headed.

"It sounds like the Feds may try to intervene. Someone is really pushing to get this project going. Keith says he's been begging for backing of some sort, but Lansing won't even return his calls now. The Michigan Militia has mobilized and has assets all over the area to help us out, which is probably our best bet," Jason explained. "You still have Dad's rifle and that other gear we got you for your twenty-first birthday, right?"

"Yes, but what are you suggesting here?"

"If the time comes, this community is prepared to defend what's theirs by whatever means necessary."

Rob didn't respond, letting Jason's words hang heavy in the air. It seemed crazy to Rob that they would be taking up arms against their own countrymen, regardless of the reason. At the same time, he recognized that if the "water management" plans drawn up by the politicians and their corporate masters didn't go precisely as calculated, it could quite literally destroy the community that had been the center of his entire existence. By following his older brother, he would be putting his life on the line, but by doing nothing he would not only still be gambling with his own future, but the futures of everyone he knew and cared about.

"Alright," he finally answered solemnly, "Just let me know when and where and I'll be there."

"We'll keep in touch. Stay ready."

CHAPTER 8

Edwards Air Force Base, California
June 22, 2030
1230 Hours PST

"Ladies and gentlemen, listen up," cracked a stiff-lipped Air Force Colonel. "We have been advised today that Washington has moved us up to DEFCON 3. We are to be on alert and ready to anticipate any attack from our foreign enemies while we are in these turbulent times at home. The President has made it quite clear that our military will not be involving itself in any domestic conflicts and will remain prepared worldwide to meet any threat leveled from a foreign adversary."

The Colonel paused to let his words sink in. Maria looked around the drab briefing room at the faces of her fellow pilots.

"What that means," the Colonel continued, "is that each of you could very well be called to action at a moment's notice. As test pilots I think it's highly unlikely your unit will be sent into battle, but I am still issuing an order to stay on base and maintain combat-readiness levels until such a time as it is no longer deemed necessary."

James turned to Maria, and she met his gaze. His eyes were wide with nervous apprehension, but she also picked up on an air of excitement in his demeanor. Well, ultimately this was what they had signed up for.

"Are there any questions?"

None of the highly disciplined and capable pilots gathered in the room made a sound. The situation was understood quite clearly. It was certainly something they had all imagined

happening someday in one capacity or another.
    "Dismissed!"

CHAPTER 9

Ishpeming, Michigan
June 25, 2030
0955 Hours EST

The call came one week later. Rob was having breakfast at Buck's, an unassuming diner on the corner of Division and Main that had been around much longer than Rob. The establishment had flourished with the good years and weathered the bad, one of many small businesses serving as the pillars that underpinned the community. It was a slow morning and only a couple other patrons filled the joint, which was currently being presided over by Buck himself. Buck was a Yooper born and bred like Rob, but with many more years of hard-bitten UP living under his belt, evidenced by his solemn, wizened features.

Rob was halfway through a plate of sunny side up eggs, crispy bacon, and generously buttered toast when he heard the tinny ascending and descending chimes of his phone ringer emitting from his jeans pocket. He quickly dabbed the greasy fingers of his right hand on a napkin and drew out his phone. When he saw Jason's name on the caller ID, he immediately slid his finger right across the bottom of the screen to answer.

"Hey," Rob uttered tersely.

"Hey." Jason responded quickly, "We need to get up to the roadblock. I just got word from Jim there's a convoy that rolled 'cross the bridge no more than 15 minutes ago. Feds most like. We think this is the response D.C. promised. Sandra's out running errands with the truck. Can you pick me up at my place?"

Jim was Jason's contact from the militia. A message to rally the troops must be spreading through the network.

"Okay, I'm at Buck's. I gotta swing by home to grab my gear then I'll be right over."

"See ya soon, bud."

Then Jason hung up.

Rob rose and pocketed his phone, then turned for the exit with alacrity, nearly sending his half-eaten breakfast onto the tiled floor. He paused at the door and gazed across at Buck, his left hand drifting down to his wallet. Buck locked eyes with him and shook his head back and forth.

"You just worry 'bout goin' doin' what you gotta do, son." Buck stated plainly in his gruff but friendly voice.

Rob gave a curt nod and was out the door, jogging towards his pickup parked on the curb. He jumped into the driver's seat, hastily buckled his seatbelt, then peeled out from his spot and navigated the small-town streets back to his house. When he arrived, he hurried through the front door and skipped down a short staircase to the partial basement where the kit he had assembled just days before was waiting.

Rob grabbed the padded mesh straps of his plate carrier and lifted it from the cabinet it was resting on up and over his head, letting the heavy vest fall across his torso. He ripped the stout Velcro upwards to open the cummerbund of the carrier and pulled the side flaps in, slotting corresponding Velcro pads in between the face of the vest and the cummerbund, then pressing down to secure the fit. The carrier held four steel core level III ballistic armor plates, two large plates covering his chest and back, and two smaller plates protecting his sides underneath his armpits. Fully loaded it weighed around twenty-five pounds, and after donning the armor Rob was left wishing he had spent more time moving around with it on to get used to the feel.

Next, he thumbed through his keyring for the key to the tall matte-black safe along the wall. Upon finding the right key, he inserted it into the lock and twisted a quarter turn to the right, allowing the hefty steel door to swing open, revealing the modest materiel within. Resting in place was the trusty AR-15 left to him by his father, adorned with a small foregrip and a simple red dot reflex sight mounted on the old but still widely popular picatinny rail system. He reached in and pulled out two sickle-shaped STANAG magazines, each already loaded with thirty 5.56x45mm 62-grain copper jacketed rounds, and slid the magazines into the pouches strapped onto the front of his plate carrier that were designed to hold them.

Rob grabbed one more fully loaded magazine and placed it on top of the safe. He then gingerly lifted the rifle, taking care not to bump the sight against the solid, unyielding walls of the safe. Wrapping his right hand around the pistol grip seated behind the trigger, he tilted it upwards, then retrieved the third magazine from its place on top of the safe. He firmly slotted it into the slightly flared magazine well, then pressing the stock against his chest he pulled back the charging handle with his left hand and then released it forwards, chambering a round.

Finally, he picked up an old surplus MICH ballistic helmet off the ground and, working the chinstrap with his fingers, fit it snugly onto his head. He knew the helmet probably wouldn't do much for him if it took a direct hit from a high-powered rifle, but it made him feel marginally less vulnerable if he actually were to end up in a gunfight. On the way to the staircase, he slung a small rucksack over his shoulder. Inside the lightweight pack was a trauma kit, a hose and bladder hydration system filled with two liters of water, some candy bars, a knife, and a roll of duct tape. He was walking back out the front door a little over sixty seconds later, echoing the minutemen of the pre-independence American colonies.

Back in his truck, Rob took off towards Jason's house. Minutes later he came to a stop in front of Jason's driveway. Jason was already standing out front, ready to go. He was wearing a helmet and body armor similar to Rob's, but instead of the t-shirt and jeans Rob had been wearing when he geared up, Jason had on camouflage fatigues, with swirling shades of green and brown that would blend seamlessly with a forest backdrop. Hanging around Jason's shoulder and upper torso on a single point sling was an intimidating black AK-99 bristling with attachments.

Based on the Kalashnikov rifle platform, known the world over for almost a century, the AK-99 was yet another variant developed a decade ago, consisting mostly of polymer and composite parts. Chambered with hard hitting 7.62x39mm ammunition, the only practical use for such a weapon in the northern reaches of Michigan was perhaps putting down a charging bull moose, but it appeared that Jason was prepared for another application altogether. Rob noticed that Jason had quite a few more items strapped or Velcroed onto his armor bearing vest. His eyes were particularly drawn to the area right below Jason's sternum, where their father's 101st Airborne unit patch was proudly adhered to the vest, bearing the screaming head of a bald eagle.

Jason stepped up to the passenger door, yanked it open, and slid into the seat. Before his seatbelt was even fully buckled, Rob depressed the accelerator pedal against the floor and took off towards the roadblock on county road KK where men and women were surely gathering from all over, prepared to meet whatever authority was being sent to attempt to disperse them. The two brothers drove wordlessly for the first fifteen minutes, joined by the sounds of tires on the road and the staticky distortion of southern rock guitar riffs on the radio. When the truck cleared downtown Marquette and turned onto county road 550, "Big Bay Road," Rob opened up the throttle and soon the speedometer needle was sitting above eighty. Who was going to pull him over? The sheriff and his deputies would all be at the blockade. They rumbled along the slight curves of the road, passing dense forest for the most part. Ten minutes out from their destination, Jason broke the silence.

"Look, Rob, you know…I think this will just go the same as last time. So, I ain't sayin' things are gonna get ugly. But…well if bullets start flying, don't try to be a hero, you hear? Keep your ass behind cover and just follow the militia boys."

"Yeah, I know," Rob stated hollowly, his mouth dry and his mind engulfed in a nervous fugue.

After a long pause Rob spoke up again.

"Where does it go from here? I mean assuming the feds and PMCs don't just plow through us with main battle tanks, like what next? So we shut them out again, but clearly elements way high up wanna force this project through. If the government's backing them, what's to stop them from showing up with a full battalion, jet planes, hell they could just hit us with hypersonic drone strikes!"

"Look Rob, you know I don't got all the answers, but first off what's the alternative? They put this pipe in and in a couple decades they suck superior dry? What do we do then? What do my kids do? If you're thinking of starting a family of your own, well think again cuz you sure ain't gonna want to stick around here once they turn it into another California desert."

"That's a bit extreme, don't you think? I mean they're getting on just fine down in the Mitten, yeah?"

"Sure, they're getting along right now, but I reckon in ten years' time they'll be hurtin' just as bad as all those poor souls out West. When this water gets taken out it doesn't come back! Not ever! Now the people of this state, we'll survive, we always do no matter what gets thrown our way, but we'll be on strict water rations for the rest of our dry dusty lives. And the kicker is, by the time we're all drained out up here, those ocean plants on the west coast will finally be up and running and they'll be sittin' pretty. See they're using us as a stop gap, to keep themselves in comfort while they sort out the mistakes they made years ago, but the cost could ruin us forever. You'd be a fool to think they'll bother to pipe all the water they stole back once we're the ones who need it.

"Okay, okay, fair enough. But I still don't see how we get out of this. Are we really going to shoot at federal officers? Fellow Americans?"

"This country, our lifestyles and livelihoods, were

founded on the principle that all men have a God-given right to freedom. It's not just our right, but our duty to resist tyranny when it infringes on the wellbeing of our community. I don't want to shoot no one regardless of who they are, but I will not allow a bunch of greedy, selfish, out-of-touch despots to destroy the future of my children and my children's children. If anyone shows up brandishing a badge performing the will of those corrupt hacks, I'd sure as hell rather talk to 'em and let 'em know what they're doing ain't right. But when words fail, bullets don't."

Rob found he had nothing more to say to that, and the pair drove on in solemn silence. As they approached the site of the barricade, vehicles were already stacked on the sides of the road, mostly pickup trucks with a few large vans. At least eighty men and a handful of women were milling around, almost all kitted out for lethal conflict. Rob pulled into an open sandy space behind the line of cars and he and Jason got out, then continued on foot towards the roadblock.

Eyeing members of the crowd, Rob saw that the equipment being worn or carried ran the full gamut. Some were dressed in simple casual or work clothes like himself, many wielding rifles but a few just wearing holstered sidearms. A number of these people were armored to some degree, but not all. On the other end of the spectrum were members of what Rob guessed must be the Michigan Militia. These men were decked out in full tactical gear; plate carriers covered in accessories like spare magazines, first aid kits, knives, scissors, tubular webbing, zip ties, and various types of grenades; ballistic helmets with integrated communications headsets; and menacing black rifles slung around necks or over shoulders.

Behind the blockade, Sheriff Halper stood with a few of his deputies, conversing with a large, bearded man whom Jason identified as the militia commander. Glancing into the surrounding woods, Rob noticed camouflaged men holding vigil in entrenched positions. The militia commander turned away from Sheriff Halper and spoke into his headset. He must have been passing on orders for his squad leaders and the message quickly trickled down to Rob and Jason. Jason had a quick chat with a heavyset militia man holding an Iraq war-era M4 Carbine then spoke to Rob.

"They say a large contingent from the ATF is on its way about thirty minutes out. They just barreled through downtown Marquette. At least a dozen armored vehicles, some MRAPs and Bearcats. They're being shadowed by a couple helicopters, too."

"Jesus, well it's really on now," muttered Rob. "So, what will we do?"

"Follow me. We'll position along the line of parked cars. Sheriff says despite the show of force, they'll back down since they still have no legal jurisdiction to be here. We need to represent some force of our own though to keep them from simply ignoring him and plowing past. The pipe could already be built by the time the corrupt courts and apathetic administrators turn the case around if we rely on bureaucracy."

And with that they settled in to wait, the tension palpable in the air.

CHAPTER 10

Powell, MI
June 25, 2030
1200 Hours EST

The passage of time felt interminably slow, but eventually Rob heard the beating of helicopter rotors and saw clouds of dust along the road heralding the approach of the ATF convoy. By now the sun was high in the sky, accompanied by a smattering of wispy clouds. A thermometer would have only read 75 degrees Fahrenheit, but in the still air with solar rays spearing down it felt much hotter. The black flies had largely run their course early this season, but mosquitos were still buzzing around to remind those present that nature always demanded blood. Rob and Jason were positioned four cars down from Sheriff Halper and the blockade. The idle chatter died out as the convoy neared, and the two helicopters eased into a languid holding pattern about 1,000 feet above. The armored vehicles decelerated, and the lead truck came to a stop about twenty feet from Halper. A moment later, a loud authoritative voice projected out from a bullhorn on the truck.

"This is the United States Bureau of Alcohol, Tobacco, Firearms and Explosives. You are all unlawfully obstructing this public road and interfering with the public traffic right of way. Clear out and leave this area immediately or we will begin making arrests."

A few seconds passed and men wearing full body armor and bearing XM5 6.8x51mm assault rifles began filing out from the rear doors of the armored transports. In addition to the rifles, the company of agents bore other heavier armaments including grenade launchers and robust ballistic shields. At this point hundreds of guns were in play on both sides, but thus far no firearms were being aimed in the direction of another person. At least none that would be visible to the other side. Sheriff Halper squeezed around the side of one of the roadblocking trucks and strode forward to address the federal agents, the massive Smith and Wesson Model 500 revolver on his hip glinting in the sun.

"I am Marquette County Sheriff Keith Halper, and this county road is under my jurisdiction. I do not find the people gathered here to be in violation of any rightful laws. They are gathered here to protest an unjust and unsanctioned breach of the Great Lakes Compact. You have no justification to be here. As the lawful authority of this land, I am ordering you to turn this convoy around and leave Marquette County."

Damn if this sheriff didn't have a pair of balls the size of grapefruits, Rob thought to himself. He spared a quick glance up at the circling choppers, a long barrel protruding from an open side door of each growling Sikorsky UH-60 Black Hawk. It wouldn't be surprising if they pulled Lon Horiuchi out of retirement for this one, Rob mused. What appeared to be the leader of the ATF contingent stepped down from the lead Mine Resistant Ambush Protected vehicle and walked a few paces towards the Sheriff, flanked by a squad of heavily armed and armored agents.

"I am Special Agent Joseph Grant with the Bureau of Alcohol, Tobacco, Firearms, and Explosives. I am here under orders of the federal government of the United States of America to investigate disorderly and economically damaging misconduct involving the potential illegal possession of restricted firearms. Now if you tell these people to disperse and remove these vehicles from the road, we can all be on our way with no further problems. If not, I *will* act with the full authority of the United States government to prosecute all parties involved as I see fit."

Halper was unphased and responded in kind.

"That's bullshit and we both know it. This is my county and my road. These citizens, acting lawfully on my land as they are, are under my protection, and I will not remand any of them to your custody without a warrant signed by a judge identifying the individual by name and listing the outstanding offenses. If you can't produce that, then leave them alone and leave my county."

Halper's voice was calm and level, but he spoke with an underlying venom that made it impossible to hide his disdain for the agents in front of him.

Grant was quick with his retort.

"Sheriff, if you are interfering with my pursuit of justice then I will be forced to place you under arrest as well."

Halper fired back.

"I don't know how I can make myself more clear. Y'all need to leave."

"Stand down Sheriff!" Grant commanded.

"The livelihoods and futures of the members of my community are being threatened by the project these people are here to protest. I do not expect any of them to stand down and I know I certainly will NOT stand down."

"Agent Jenkins, take this man into custody."

An indistinct agent, facial features hidden by a black balaclava and ballistic goggles, took a hesitant step forward from the group.

Halper stuck his right leg out straight, knee locked, then placed the heel of his boot on the ground and dragged it about a yard along the earth, drawing a line in the sandy dirt of the road. He then took a couple steps back from the line and plainly stated:

"If any of y'all take so much as a single step beyond that line, I will consider it a threat to my personal safety and liberty, and the safety and liberty of the good citizens around me. I will react accordingly."

He let those words hang in the air. The Black Hawks were still buzzing ominously overhead, but the gathered assortment of armed men and women guarding the roadblock must have had the agents outnumbered at least two to one. It was clear that Agent Grant was not used to having his authority challenged, at least not without grave consequence to the offending party, and Rob wasn't sure that he would back down.

Grant appeared to struggle to keep his cool as he forced his next words out through a snarling grimace.

"Agent Jenkins. Take. This. Man. Into. Custody."

Jenkins took another unsure step towards Halper. Halper cut an imposing figure, standing tall in the afternoon sun, hands placed squarely on his hips. His crisply pressed brown shirt bulged at the seams as it struggled to conceal the combined size of his powerful chest and plates of ceramic body armor. From his Stetson to his boots, Halper exuded pure "don't-fuck-with-me" confidence. For a moment, Halper's expression turned sad, almost pleading, as he locked eyes with Jenkins and said to him "Son, don't do it."

Jenkins glanced back at Grant, then walked towards Halper, slinging his rifle over his shoulder and unlinking a pair of handcuffs from his utility belt. Halper stood, unflinching. Jenkins stopped a foot away from the line Halper had drawn, appeared to mull over his situation for a second, then took one step past the line.

In a flash Halper had his oversized revolver out of the holster and extended lock-arm towards Jenkins. He didn't hesitate, he squeezed the trigger right away. The huge-barreled handgun boomed like a cannon as Halper planted a .500 magnum round dead center of Jenkins's upper torso. The man was visibly lifted off his feet and his body flew backwards, landing halfway between Halper and the ATF agents. Halper's arm flexed back at a forty-five-degree angle, taking in the recoil. Plumes of smoke curled out from the barrel then wisped forward to fill the vacuum where the large magnum bullet had displaced air on its lethal course.

The hundreds of gunmen present were momentarily stunned still, all except for Halper who immediately spun to his side and dove for cover behind a nearby truck. The next shots came from one of the helicopters up high, rifle rounds kicked up dirt as they chased Halper's dash to the truck. A sniper on the chopper deck surely had Halper in his crosshairs but must've been so taken aback by Halper's speed and violence of action that he was unable to bring down the venerable sheriff.

To say all hell broke loose next would be an understatement. Guns came up, any safeties that were still on were quickly flicked off, and the gun-toting warriors began emptying magazines as fast as they could into the opposition. ATF agents flopped prone or took what cover they could behind the sizable armored vehicles, while protesters and militia men pressed into trucks, trees, and boulders. The overwhelming chatter of staccato rifle shots from the militia was nearly matched by the fully automatic fire of the ATF agents and their military spec XM5s.

Rob only had a split second to regret leaving his ear protection behind as he was fully deafened by the outpouring of gunfire surrounding him. He couldn't bring himself to sight down on any individual person, but he still unleashed round after high-velocity round into the mass of the ATF convoy arrayed before him. Screams of pain, shouted commands, and unintelligible war cries began to pierce the uproar of the ordnance being expended.

As Rob ducked down to reload, he witnessed ruby red arterial spray coat the ground as a man behind the next truck over caught a round to the neck. A woman farther down the line popped up over the cab of a rusty green pickup and pumped out round after round from a long, blocky FN FAL before return fire spun her to the ground. Combatants were going down on both sides as hot lead met armor plates or flesh. Some got back up, some didn't.

The Sheriff and the militia commander had a strong firing position set up along the blockade, and in conjunction with the remaining resistors arrayed along the side of the road and up in the surrounding woods, they had the ATF contingent caught in an enfilading field of fire. The ATF forces, utilizing the heavily armored trucks and ballistic shields, had a hardened position of their own and were giving as good as they got. The smell of gunpowder soon permeated the air. Deadly fire spat from the helicopter gunners, putting down militiamen with no way to cover from such an angle of elevation. That problem was promptly dealt with as someone from the militia opened up with a squad automatic weapon. The stream of sustained high cycle fire caused one chopper to peel back and dip below some nearby hills, while the other was chased away by a torrent of semi-automatic rifle rounds.

It was a wonder that the ATF forces were standing up against the withering fusillade, but they fought back with their own force equalizers. Rob heard a low *fwump*, barely audible over the chaos raging around, the telltale sound of a grenade being launched. A projectile effusing thick white smoke landed behind the militia battle line, a few yards from where Rob was crouched down, fumbling to insert a new magazine into his rifle.

"Gas, gas, gas!" Jason shouted in his ear. "We gotta move-" he sputtered, already starting to cough from the noxious chlorobenzalmalononitrile. The CS gas, while non-lethal, greatly diminished the combat capabilities of those caught in its baleful cloud and dispersing the gas among the militia was allowing the ATF to gain an edge in fire superiority.

Rob finally slammed the magazine home, pressed down on the bolt catch to release the bolt, and felt a metallic thunk as the bolt slammed forward, chambering the next round. He then sprinted in a low crouch for a spot a few cars down where a squad of militiamen were fighting unimpeded by the gas cloud. Holding his rifle in front of him by the fore and rear grips, perpendicular to his body, he squeezed off a couple shots as he moved to cover. He was almost at the next truck, preparing to slide into place, then all of a sudden he was on his back. For a moment he felt nothing, then his left side was enveloped by oppressive pain.

Rob gasped for air, realizing he must have been hit. It

didn't hurt quite as much as the movies and books made it seem, but maybe he was already dying, and the pain was fading as his lifeforce leaked out from his body back into the universe that created him. A gloved hand reached out and grabbed his ankle, then he was roughly dragged into cover behind the truck, his helmeted cranium bouncing off the hard ground.

The man who had dragged him behind the truck quickly scanned Rob's body. After noting the ragged impact site on the side of his vest, he wedged a hand up underneath Rob's shirt and plate carrier then pulled it out. The glove came out clean, no blood.

"You're good!" the man shouted before bringing up his rifle and getting back in the fight.

Rob's side was in agony, and he was still sucking in breaths. It felt like he'd taken a gut punch from a gorilla trained by Mike Tyson. Leaning up against the rear tire of the truck he had arrived at, he noticed the relentless cacophony of gunfire had dissipated significantly, replaced by the lower roar of engines. He bent down and peaked underneath the undercarriage of the truck he was sheltering behind and saw black armored vehicles reversing back down the dusty road.

"Ceasefire! Ceasefire! Ceasefire!" The man next to him called out, a similar call echoing through the ranks of militia fighters. The commander must have put the call out over the net and those militia members keyed into the communications channel were spreading the word to everyone else. Shouts of "Medical! Medical!" and "Over here!" rang across the abruptly vacated killing field.

Gunsmoke mixed with traces of CS gas hung heavy in the air. The sun was partially obscured, although warm rays of sunshine pierced through the veil of martial exhaust. Inhaling put an acrid, bitter taste on Rob's tongue. The percussive din of sustained rifle fire was now replaced by cries of agony from the wounded, and more haunting moans of the dying. For the most part though, all Rob heard was a loud persistent ringing. He had to concentrate hard to avoid being overcome with dizziness. He eased himself up onto his feet, slightly hunched over from the dull pain in his side. His mind was swimming, a combination of mental shock at the abrupt descent into brutality and the physical sensory overload of combat. He thought they must have been fighting for an hour, maybe longer, but when he held up his wrist, his watch face claimed only a couple minutes had passed. Through the haze, one thought bubbled to the surface. *Find Jason.*

Rob felt hollow as he stumbled across the dirt road-turned battlefield. His thoughts felt disconnected from his body, and his field of view seemed to have narrowed as if his eyes were now set back farther into his head. Militiamen and other resistors were scurrying around, dragging bodies into a triage line. The ATF had retreated in a hurry, leaving the lead armored truck and a number of injured at the scene. Wounded fighters were being arranged in order of the severity of their injuries, no distinction being made based on which side they had been on moments before. Militia medics were now fighting with every tool in their arsenal to save civilian protesters and federal agents alike.

Rob walked along the triage line, passing the green and gray hued forms of fallen militia interspersed with those of black clad ATF agents. Near the front of the line many of those forms were gently stirring or writhing around, but as he trudged on, more and more of the figures were deathly still. At the end of the line his eye was drawn to a spot of white. He stopped and stared as his brain processed the small white shape, which soon coalesced into the visage of a bald eagle, its beak held wide open. The screaming eagle.

Rob flopped down to the motionless body upon which the screaming eagle patch was proudly displayed. Jason's face was barely recognizable, one half partially caved in and smothered in a vermillion layer of blood. Rob searched desperately for a pulse, tried to feel for a soft exhalation of air emitting from Jason's bloodstained lips, but came up empty. He got up, took a few steps, then fell back down to his knees and began vomiting uncontrollably.

CHAPTER 11

Edwards Air Force Base, California
June 27, 2030
0450 Hours PST

Maria was jolted out of the austere cot in her spartan quarters by a shrill, penetrating alarm klaxon. The dark room was bathed in dim red light. She checked her watch: 0452 hours. A message played in between blaring tones of the siren.

"All flight personnel, report to your stations and prep for immediate deployment. I repeat, all flight personnel report to your stations and prep for immediate deployment."

They'd gone through drills like this on the base every so often, some announced, some unannounced, but on an instinctual level Maria knew this time it was the real deal. She slid on her flight suit and grabbed her operations go-bag, packed and ready with her flying kit. She threw open the door and took off at a brisk jog down the hallway towards the hangar. A few other pilots in her wing were already out and heading in the same direction. A door flew open in front of her, and she nearly collided with James. James paused and made a twirling "after you" motion with his right hand and Maria continued on, with James at her heels.

"So, this is it yeah?" James queried, "I think we're gonna finally see some action."

"I think so, too," Maria somberly agreed.

"Well, I'm comin' fangs out for whoever the poor bastards are that we're up against. I don't know about you, but I can't wait to paint some kill markings on the side of my Storm Crow."

Maria considered his attitude for a moment. She wasn't so bloodthirsty herself, but she had to admit she was itching for a taste of real air combat. The training sims had gotten more and more realistic, but in the end, there was no truer test of one's piloting prowess than going toe-to-toe with an enemy pilot in a live fire no-holds-barred duel with lethal intent. Maria suspected that all of her colleagues, even the most composed and level-headed of the bunch, held a desire, on some level at least, to take their birds to the skies in a real battle. By nature, fighter jocks tended to be confident and cocksure, always looking for a way to test their skills and prove themselves. When you flew a hundred-million-dollar machine through the stratosphere at Mach 2 with the firepower to level a city block at your fingertips, it inevitably got to your head.

The pair rounded the corner to where the ready room was located and were met by a Major blocking the entrance, waving them onwards down towards the hangar.

"Go straight to the tarmac. You'll be briefed in the air. We need you wheels up ASAFP!" the Major proclaimed in a loud voice just under a shout. James gave her a puzzled look but then shrugged and moved on.

That was odd, thought Maria. They'd never take off without a briefing and flight plan. What could conceivably be going on? Her mind began to race with possibilities, but the rational section of her brain, a blade of discipline deeply forged by years of military service took over. Focus on the task at hand. Get to the plane, get in the sky, then get answers.

She ran out onto the tarmac and into the cool morning air. The sunlight was just beginning to slip out from behind the scattered, craggy peaks to the east. Most of the aircraft were already outside the hangar, being tended to by mechanics and flight techs. She heard the deafening roar of jet engines as fighters began taking off farther down the runway. A flight tech jogged up and pushed a meal replacement shake and a caffeine tablet into her hands. She thanked him and he dashed off to provide similar vittles to the next pilot down. This gave her the feeling she was in for a long flight. Knowing that she would need fuel just as much as her aircraft would, she dutifully slurped down the shake and popped the caf tab.

Maria stepped up to her jet just as the ground crew was finishing up. She gave them a crisp nod and they gave her quick lazy salutes in return. One of the crewmen whom she recognized from the mess addressed her:

"She's all set for ya. Good luck up there."

"I don't suppose you know..." Maria started to ask, but before she could finish, she saw the man definitively nodding his head back and forth.

Maria climbed up the small, wheeled staircase the crewman had positioned next to the cockpit, then hopped into her flight chair. She keyed the cockpit shut and began running through her pre-flight checklist as the crew pulled out the wheel chocks, pushed the stairs away, and scurried off for the next job. The F-25 Storm Crow was loaded out with six AIM-260 JATMs, two AIM-9 Sidewinders, and four 600-gallon fuel drop tanks. As predicted, she was going to be flying quite a distance. She noted her M61A2 Vulcan rotary cannon was topped off with 500 rounds of 20mm SAPHEI shells, semi-armor piercing high explosive incendiary, capable of ripping through the metallic hide of any fighter craft in operation.

Maria taxied out towards the nearest runway strip and began communicating with the control tower. She got a heading from them, due northwest, and when she was cleared for takeoff, she lit up her engines and thundered down the runway. As she climbed into the atmosphere, she searched for her wingmates and began to link up with the larger fighter group forming up over the central valley. She was staring at the silent sunrise when a commanding voice broke in through her headset.

"All elements of the 412th Wing, this is General David Armstrong. We are receiving reports of a substantial group of hostile aircraft over the Bering Sea. Patrolling elements from the Fifth Carrier Strike Group called it in one hour ago and transmitted data indicating a strength of at least one hundred aircraft before we lost contact with them. The Fourth and Fifth Carrier groups are mobilizing in response, but we are also scrambling units across the west coast. We believe this to be a precursor move to gain air superiority by a foreign nation and are expecting heavy resistance. We will meet this threat with every resource at our disposal. You are to burn hard towards the Gulf of Alaska where a refueling team will meet you before you enter what we anticipate will be the theater of battle. Godspeed."

CHAPTER 12

Presidential Emergency Operations Center, Washington, D.C.
June 27, 2030
0755 Hours EST

"Can somebody tell me who the hell these guys are?"

The President and a group of his closest advisors and generals were gathered in the highly reinforced bunker deep underneath the East Wing of the White House. There was an air of sullen anxiety in the room, and the President's indignant irritation was becoming evident. The National Security Advisory spoke up.

"Sir, Putin is denying having anything to do with this, and based on our intelligence we have strong reason to believe him. The Chinese are denying it as well-"

"Nobody else on this planet could assemble this kind of airpower, and it sure as hell ain't Martians!" The President cut in.

A woman from the Office of Naval Intelligence chimed in, "Mr. President, our analysts have ID'd with a high degree of confidence both Russian Sukhoi aircraft and Chinese Chengdu craft from the radar signature transmissions acquired by our scouting patrol. While this doesn't give us definitive proof one way or another, we know the Chinese maintain Russian-made models in their active fleet whereas the Russians only field aircraft of domestic manufacture. Then again, it could be an intentional deception..." She trailed off.

"Get me Xi on the line NOW!" The President declared, barely managing to keep his cool.

"Sir we've been trying, we've reached one of his ministers

who is saying he is currently indisposed, but denies knowing anything about a major military operation," a presidential aide answered.

"I'm doing my damndest to keep us off the brink of a civil war here and this bastard thinks he can come in and catch us with our pants down? We need to let him know that our external military capabilities are unaffected, especially our *nuclear* arsenal." The President placed a cold emphasis on the word "nuclear."

Nobody spoke for a moment while the President appeared to consider his next words. Slowly he resumed his chain of thought.

"General Attenborough...your people have orbital strike trajectories drawn up and ready, I presume?"

"Yes, sir."

"I want a single nuclear warhead unlocked and ready for satellite launch. We'll hit one of their remote military installations in the Gansu province. If we fire a Greyhound there's no way they can stop it, and they can't hit us back in any meaningful way through our SDI field. If Xi doesn't want to listen to words, we'll send him a clear message with our actions."

A clamor of voices followed, both assenting and dissenting opinions making themselves vociferously heard.

"That's absurd. You can't!"

"Good move, sir. We have to show absolute strength here."

"No, no, no..."

"It's about time we reminded the world who the top dog is."

The President broke the hubbub with a sharp "Alright!"

"General," He continued, addressing the decorated United States Space Force commander, "Get that missile armed and on standby, if we don't hear from Xi in ten minutes, we launch."

"Wait."

A flinty, authoritative decree came from the back corner. Heads turned to focus on the steely visage of the CIA Director. After it was clear that he had everyone's attention, he spoke further.

"We can't do that. Our latest primary source intelligence from an operator we nearly lost in the Philippines suggests that the Chinese have completed development of a class five hypersonic rocket delivery system. We don't believe they are aware of this yet, but if they were to fire one of those at us, our defense network would only have a marginal probability of stopping it before it reached its target. Our countermeasure project is still months from completion. If we got into a nuclear engagement with the Chinese right now, it could prove disastrous."

The calamitous implication of his words hung in the air.

"Why am I just now hearing about this?" The President demanded.

"With all due respect, Mr. President," the director responded, "The report crossed your desk two months ago. I placed it there myself."

"I've spent nearly every waking hour this year trying to keep the states from tearing each other apart, I don't have time to spend sifting through pages of memos and essays!" The President retorted.

"Regardless, sir, that is the situation as it stands. We cannot initiate a nuclear strike against China."

"Then what *are* our options?"

The room fell silent. A few seconds later the Secretary of Defense softly stated,

"Sir, we have to win the fight in the air."

CHAPTER 13

20,000 feet over the Gulf of Alaska
June 27, 2030
0800 Hours AKST

The sun had burned off most of the cloud cover, and the high-altitude skies were a deep savoy blue. The midair refueling had gone smoothly, but Maria could sense an underlying air of unease and anxious anticipation in all the radio comms. As her squadron approached the rendezvous point over the north Pacific, a sprawling array of aircraft began to take shape before her. In all, her unit had arrived with forty-nine air superiority fighter jets, including twenty of the next generation Storm Crows. It looked as if over 300 friendly aircraft were gathered in the skies around her, more than she had ever seen before even in a Red Flag exercise.

The force consisted mostly of advanced tactical fighters: F-35A Lightning IIs, F-22A Raptors, and even some old F-15 Eagles. There was also a large contingent of Navy F/A-18 Super Hornets, and a number of Valkyrie drones dutifully following some of the lead jets. Towards the rear of the expansive formation were a variety of support and utility craft, primarily for electronic warfare and command and control. She shivered at the thought of so much hardware and firepower, but what really sent a chill down her spine was when she tried to picture what foe could garner such a response.

Her squadron was designated with callsign "Hammer," Maria and James taking on the battlefield monikers of Hammer Four and Five respectively.

"Hammer squadron, this is Overlord Actual, you're just in time. Our long-range scans indicate that we'll be in range of the hostile air fleet in ten minutes. Stay tight with us. Our support wing is casting an ECM bubble. When I give the word, I want all BVR missiles off the rails as fast as you pull good locks. We know they're running strong countermeasures of their own, but we should have the volume to overwhelm them."

Maria did her best to stay calm and steel her resolve for the battle ahead. She'd been through plenty of simulated engagements and was familiar with all aspects of air-to-air combat, but now that the enemy was real, she found herself getting a jittery sensation she hadn't felt since flight school. Before she had time to dwell too much on the approaching conflict, targeting information and commands began to pour in over her tactical channel.

"Overlord Two for Hammer One."

"Go for Hammer One."

"We're highlighting targets for you now - check sector E-12. Hold formation with Tiger and Shark squadrons but be ready to split off and address threats to sector J-10."

"Good copy."

"Happy hunting. Overlord Two out."

CHAPTER 14

20,000 feet over the Gulf of Alaska
June 27, 2030
0830 Hours AKST

Onboard a Boeing E-3 Sentry command and control jet, Lieutenant Colonel Charles Yarnell was giving everything he had to stay on top of the developing combat space and direct his units appropriately. He had seen real combat before over the skies of the Middle East, but nothing compared to this scale. He had also never gone up against an opponent outside of training that had the same electronic warfare capacity that this enemy seemed to possess. At the moment, every neuron in his brain was firing in support of his ability to command his 547 aircraft to victory against this unknown foe.

"Sir, General Attenborough is on the line," One of his communications officers informed him.

"Put him through."

Moments later the gruff voice of the venerable general came through his headset.

"Lieutenant Colonel, the President would like a status update on the situation up there."

"Yes, sir, we're starting to break through their wide band jamming. It looks like a couple hundred fighters at least. I'd bet my life that these are Chi-Comms. We're seeing tons of signature matches. We'll be engaging with long range missiles and drone assets in under two minutes. I don't think they anticipated this response from us, so we should be able to handle this easily."

"Thank you, Lieutenant Colonel. Give 'em hell."

"Yes, sir."

Yarnell turned back to the holographic display of the airspace, where icons for individual enemy elements were beginning to resolve themselves from the mass of unconfirmed radar returns. He began barking out commands.

"Targeting, start distributing weapons locks. Make sure our jamming stays tight and begin walking up our EWs. Four, have Griffin and Beach divert zero-two-zero degrees and throttle up ten percent."

"Sir," a radar tech called out, "I've gotten through the sweep jamming and modulated their pulses. We should be getting a much clearer picture-"

"My god..." Yarnell's jaw dropped. There's...there's over one thousand contacts."

"Yes, sir, that's...that's a lot, sir." The tech stammered, speechless himself.

"Are those troop transports back there?" Yarnell queried.

"Yes, sir. I believe so."

"Christ, it's an all-out invasion force. Get me the general right now!"

CHAPTER 15

20,000 feet over the Gulf of Alaska
June 27, 2030
0832 Hours AKST

Maria was no stranger to the intricate dance of modern air combat between two adversaries each possessing current generation tech. They had trained and simulated such engagements ad nauseam. All the while, she had fully expected that if and when she ever saw real action, it would be swatting some two-generation old Russian surplus jet like a fly over a backwater third world country with no air defense to speak of. No more interactive than pushing a button on a vending machine. The imminent confrontation she was now facing would surely prove to be a more delicate and demanding endeavor.

The first stage of the fight had already started hours ago: the informational warfare portion. Each side was playing a high-level chess game with onboard electronics, both scanning and jamming the opponent to try to ascertain the exact location and nature of the opposition while masking their own disposition. Maria's jet's computer was linked in with those of her allies as they continued building a better and better picture of the enemy aircraft in an effort to determine the best tactical approach and grab positive radar locks for missile deployment. They were about to enter the second stage, where the ordnance started flying.

Her squadron leader came on the line, "Hammer One to all Hammer elements. You have your targets. Fire when ready."

This was met with a chorus of "Fox Three" calls as Maria and her wingmates cut loose a swarm of AIM-260 JATMs. After launching, the allied craft began pulling back, trying to stay out of range of the enemy force, which they appeared to have a slight technological advantage over. The enemy fighters soon closed the gap and began returning fire, although not without taking losses in the process.

"Splash one bandit!" Maria exclaimed, confirming one of her missiles had taken out an enemy fighter. The excitement wore off quickly as the onboard alarm alerting her that she was being actively tracked by multiple radar locks sounded out. The massive orderly formations of fighters on either side quickly devolved into helter-skelter clouds of aircraft pulling high-G maneuvers to avoid being taken out by the explosive warheads tracking them.

Maria looked out through her cockpit canopy and saw fiery streaks of missiles lancing out through the airspace around her. It struck her that these were live munitions, and the price paid for taking a hit could very well be her life. Most of the contrails traced paths well past the group of friendly aircraft, missiles losing their locks either to radar jamming or outmaneuvering. These payloads would rain down harmlessly over the vast Pacific Ocean. Clouds of chaff tore other missiles off their course and fooled them into premature termination, dotting the sky with smoky fireballs. As the onslaught of missiles picked up, some began to find their mark.

"Hammer Three punching out!" her squadmate screamed, an edge of hysteria to his voice, before he pulled the ejection handle that would send his flight chair rocketing up through the canopy and into the thin air, to hopefully drift down on a parachute to the relative safety of the ocean below. It was certainly safer than being strapped to a flaming jet engine spiraling out of control, but Maria understood that rescue was far from guaranteed for anyone ejecting in this scenario.

Maria turned her focus back to her own situation. Her vision narrowed as she pulled a hard corner, throwing one missile off her trail. She had to dump chaff immediately afterwards as a second projectile with her in its sights came within seconds of permanently clipping her wings.

"Got one!" she heard James announce triumphantly over the comm.

"Hammer Two ejecting!" another pilot in Maria's squad quickly blurted out before that pilot's craft began to arc down towards the ocean far below.

CHAPTER 16

20,000 feet over the Gulf of Alaska
June 27, 2030
0845 Hours AKST

"Where are those units from the First and Seventh?" Yarnell snapped out.

"Sir elements from the First are still thirty minutes out, the Seventh is over an hour away."

Reinforcements were on the way, but the fight could well be over for his force by the time they arrived. His pilots had made a good showing so far, maintaining positive kill ratios, but he had lost almost half of his fighters and the sheer numerical advantage of the opposing force would eventually overcome his individually superior units. Yarnell knew that pulling back and ceding space to the enemy was not an option. If they were able to press in over the mainland, they could start landing troops on U.S. soil. Yarnell and every one of his aviators would go down in flames before they allowed that to happen. He had to buy time for backup, but without retreating his options were limited. They would just have to take the enemy head on and give them one hell of a fight.

"Sir, our lead fighters are approaching visual range on hostile craft. Are we committing?" a young tactical officer asked.

"Affirmative. All elements are to close in and engage."

"Sir, what about our rear guard?"

"I want them forward as well. We need every gun we can get on the line."

A contingent of fighters had been hanging back to provide

security for the ponderous support planes, one of which was serving as Yarnell's base of command. Ordering them up was a big risk as it would leave his support fleet exposed to any hostile fighter jets that managed to break through, but Yarnell decided he could not afford to leave any combat capable craft out of the approaching dogfight. He would do his utmost to continue to issue commands to his fighter wings, taking advantage of his full spectrum picture of the battlefield, but he knew that once the two sides became involved in close quarters dogfighting, any high-level tactics would completely break down. His pilots would have to rely on their wits and their wingmen to survive.

CHAPTER 17

20,000 feet over the Gulf of Alaska
June 27, 2030
0848 Hours AKST

A relative lull had fallen across the airspace after the initial barrage of exchanged missiles slackened. Maria's heart raced as black dots in the distance began to materialize into enemy planes before her eyes. She was torn between dueling senses of overwhelming thrill and dread. BFM combat was admittedly the most exhilarating aspect of flying an advanced fighter jet, yet she had already borne witness to myriad sobering reminders that this fight was real, and the stakes were life and death.

"Hammer One to all Hammer elements, stay tight and engage by pairs. Leopard and Panther squadrons are breaking right at heading two-six-five. We'll stagger behind and cover their tails."

They were under a minute from the merge, the point at which planes from both sides would move into each other's airspace and the real dogfighting would begin. Already, hazy white contrails of infrared homing missiles were gridding the skies. Maria had two AIM-9 Sidewinders remaining of her initial missile complement but she was holding onto them to make them really count. She scanned her instruments and braced herself for the G-forces she was about to endure, then the enemy was upon them.

"Bandits ten o'clock. Break left!" James called out.

"On 'em," Maria called back.

She jerked the flight stick and banked left to acquire a

target. Before her, the dark form of a fighter jet was yawning through a wide turn, attempting to get behind Leopard squad. She rolled into its wake and began to line up on it. The craft barely reacted, sliding into a series of predictable basic evasion maneuvers. This must be a drone, considered Maria. Any human pilot trained to the level of piloting a current generation fighter craft, regardless of their country of origin, would know unpredictability was paramount in shaking an enemy off your tail.

Maria gave it no more thought and drew a bead on the craft. A set of holographic lines forming a funnel danced around on her heads-up display indicated the calculated trajectory that her 20mm cannon rounds would take when fired. Seconds later she locked up the enemy craft with her radar targeting computer, and a solid dot appeared where the computer predicted she should aim and fire to achieve a hit on the foe. After lolling back and forth a couple times, she drifted her reticule over the dot.

"Guns guns guns."

Maria gave the trigger on her joystick a solid one-second squeeze. The Vulcan cannon roared and spat a line of 1,580 grain SAPHEI rounds at over 1,000 meters per second towards her target. The drone soaked up multiple hits then split apart in a smoky explosion.

"Boola boola!" she whooped.

"Good kill, Slim," James said.

"More bandits, four o'clock," came the voice of Hammer One.

"Engaging."

"Got one on my tail!"

"Someone tag this bastard!"

Maria clenched her core tight and cornered hard to acquire a darting craft hot on the heels of Hammer Six, nearly stalling her own craft in the process. At this distance she could clearly make out the profile of a Chengdu J-20. She tagged the J-20 in her targeting display and snap-fired a sidewinder.

"Fox Two."

The J-20 rolled to the right while letting off a spurt of cannon fire. The tracers tracked towards Hammer Six but were abruptly cut off as Maria's sidewinder detonated on top of the Chinese fighter jet, enveloping the plane and pilot in a white-hot ball of flame and ending the threat to Hammer Six.

"Wahow, shit hot Hammer Four."

"Scratch one bandito."

"Heavy contact one-four-five!"

Maria noted about a dozen hostile planes advancing on Hammer squad.

"Hammer One for Panther. Can we get some support?"

"Hammer One this is Panther Two. We're tied up, can't break through."

"Hammer for Leopard. How copy?"

No response came.

"Hammer squad, looks like we're on our own. Form up on me, and let's try to pull them back towards Gamma sector."

The situation had taken a turn for the worse with a large group of Shenyang J-11s bearing down on them. As the enemy fighters caught up to what remained of her squadron, the frenetic struggle turned frantic. Hammer Six blew one fighter out of the sky with a sidewinder but was bracketed by cannon fire from two more fighters and his craft was torn apart. A trio of friendly F-35s joined the fray, teaming with Hammer One to flip the tables on a pair of J-11s. Maria soon lost track of their location as she and James found themselves hounded by four enemy fighters.

"Slim, cut right and I'll slice that bandit off your tail," James quickly spoke.

Maria followed his call, and pulled across his path, dragging one pursuing enemy straight into James's sights and an early grave. Maria still had another hostile trailing her, but she saw James was now tangling with two enemies of his own. Maria quickly adjusted her angle of attack and fell in directly behind one pursuer who was tunneling in on James, likely on the verge of lining up a kill shot. Maria lined up beautifully herself, staring right up the enemy's tailpipe. With a quick call of "Fox Two" she sent a boresighted sidewinder screaming towards the hostile craft. The target jet popped flares in reaction, but it was too late to matter as the sidewinder detonated right on target, incinerating the hostile fighter. Bits of scrap metal pinged off Maria's fuselage as she careened through the cloud of fire.

The second fighter on James was coming at him from another angle though and got off a ferocious volley. The tracers passed by alarmingly close to James's cockpit.

"Slim, he's right on me!" James cried out.

"Stay cool, Joker. I'll get the bastard."

Maria came around as fast as she could while still maneuvering to shake off her own pursuer. James was pulling a hard turn, but the enemy J-11 was on him like glue. Maria struggled to draw the craft into her sights. James cut his angle of attack hard and vectored his thrust to quickly adjust his direction in a post-stall maneuver, but the enemy pilot seemed to have read his mind and mirrored his actions. Maria looped above the two jets in a turn so tight it darkened her vision. The loop was drawing her cannon reticle right towards the dot that predicted where she needed to lead her shots to make contact with the enemy craft.

Maria was seconds away from pulling the trigger when the J-11 caught James's Storm Crow with a burst of cannon shells, piercing through his cockpit canopy and sending his fighter on a terminal trajectory into the waters far below.

Maria squeezed out a long burst, delivering swift retribution to the J-11, but watched helplessly as the smoking Storm Crow James had been flying dropped down out of her field of view. No visible ejection. Maria felt a sinking sensation in her gut but stifled any emotional response to keep up her situational awareness. The final J-11 had been keeping up with her, but thus far she had been able to stay just ahead of it.

She turned and jinked wildly, methodically executing a series of dramatic movements in a dogged effort to shake her foe. If the enemy fighter still had any missiles left, she would have been taken down long ago, so it was just guns on guns for now. She scanned her display and saw she had seventy-five rounds remaining, just enough for one solid burst. She would have to make it count. She pushed her Storm Crow to its limits, employing every trick she had ever learned and even some new ones that came to her in the moment. Nothing could break the deadlock. If she was lucky, maybe an ally would come along and rid her of the threat. Likewise, she realized she had already been lucky that all of the other enemy fighters in her locale were occupied themselves.

Maria determined that she had to end this now. If nothing else, if she kept up the stalemate of aggressive maneuvering, she would run out of fuel and her craft would fall lifelessly from the sky. She decided she would just have to commit everything and burn as hard as she could all at once. Either line up and tag her opponent, or black out trying. Maria disengaged the angle of attack limiter on her flight stick and took a quick breath, then began pulling back hard on the stick. She immediately felt the crushing G-forces on her body, but as she watched clouds of white and black spin past through her cockpit canopy, she saw the enemy gradually drift into her field of view. The enemy pilot must have seen what she was doing and began to match her turn, slowing the rate at which she was acquiring him, but she responded in kind by pulling harder on the flight stick, relentlessly closing the angle.

Maria's vision narrowed as she began to pull in excess of eleven Gs. She could feel the frame of her fighter trembling under the forces being applied. Either her body of flesh or her jet's body of metal would soon fail, but she pressed on. She could barely make out any sounds and she was losing strength in her grip, but her crosshair was millimeters away from lining up on the enemy fighter. Through her tenuous grasp on conscious thought, Maria registered that her crosshair was in position, and diverted every last active bit of motive force in her body towards squeezing the trigger as tightly as she could.

Flames erupted from the rotating barrels of her Vulcan cannon, and a hot stream of 20mm rounds stitched across the enemy fighter's fuselage. The armor-piercing tips punched through the thin structure of the aircraft, delivering their small incendiary payload within the guts of the craft. Electronics sparked and fuel ignited, shredding the J-11 from the inside out.

Maria eased back on the flight stick, on the verge of passing out. Awareness flooded back in time for her to catch the glint of the enemy fighter falling out of the sky.

"Alpha Mike Foxtrot." She muttered.

Adios, motherfucker.

Maria took in her surroundings. All of her wingmates from Hammer squadron were gone. She couldn't find any friendly signatures at all on her short-range scanner. What she did notice was another trio of J-11s heading straight for her. Low on fuel, out of guns, but still brimming with fury and force of will, Maria determined that if these guys wanted to bring her down, she was going to make them work for it. Her body ached from long hours in the cockpit coupled with the nearly nonstop force vectors tugging on her body during the previous thirty minutes, but she nonetheless lit off her afterburners and angled in for a hard dive.

Keeping an eye on the three aggressor aircraft, she witnessed the group quickly disperse before the lead craft burst into a cloud of debris. She watched as more missiles streaked towards the remaining two fighters, quickly catching them and enveloping them in lethal explosions.

"Hammer Four, this is Zebra One. Looks like you could use some help," a fresh and energetic voice crackled through her headset. "Sorry we're late, it was a long flight. What's your sit-rep?"

Maria hesitated for a moment, processing the situation before she responded. "I'm Bingo on fuel and Winchester on ammo, don't think there's much more I can do up here."

"Alright, get your ass back to rally point Charlie. We'll take it from here."

Maria noted that "we" referred to an entire wing of F-22 Raptors burning hard towards her position. All at once a nearly overwhelming wave of fatigue swept through Maria, and in a daze, she set a course that would take her in the direction of the nearest designated landing strip.

CHAPTER 18

20,000 feet over the Gulf of Alaska
June 27, 2030
0925 Hours AKST

Lieutenant Colonel Yarnell struggled to calm his breathing and bring his heart rate back down. His first taste of combat had very nearly been his last. Reinforcements from the central United States as well as a carrier group patrolling off the shores of South Korea had arrived just in time. The initial combat force assembled under his command was all but wiped out and he had lost nearly half his support units as the Chinese fighters broke through the back line and began an open season on the relatively slow and defenseless auxiliary aircraft. It looked like one enemy fighter had been angling for his own E-3 before being taken out by an allied long-range missile.

"Get me in touch with the Coast Guard," he demanded to the crew of support officers and technicians working frantically within the cramped airborne command center. "We need to mobilize search and rescue teams right now, there must be over two hundred airmen down in the water."

A new voice crackled over his radio.

"Griffin One for Overlord, Griffin One for Overlord."

"Go for Overlord Actual," Yarnell responded directly.

"We're tracking about a hundred retreating enemy aircraft here. They look to be unarmed. Please advise how you would like us to proceed."

That must be the enemy's own command and supporting fleet, as well as the transports containing ground troops.

"Try to herd a couple back here intact if you can. Terminate all the rest."

Yarnell knew it was unlikely any of the enemy craft would surrender, likely under orders from the Chinese government not to be taken alive and thus not offer any opportunity to link the Chinese Communist Party directly to the attack. The enemy aircraft had been scrubbed of all markings and were not transmitting any IFF codes, but he knew they had to have come from China. It seemed that the world was in for a turbulent time ahead, but Yarnell couldn't devote any mental energy to contemplating the fallout of this attack. He had much more exigent matters to process.

PART II

CHAPTER 19

Marquette, Michigan
December 20, 3031
1520 Hours EST

Light flakes of snow were drifting lazily to the ground, as if some celestial entity up above was sprinkling sugar over the town below. This dusting coupled with the ubiquitous Christmas lights lent an idyllic holiday atmosphere to the streets of Marquette, but all of that was lost on Rob as he navigated the slushy roads in his pickup truck.

The events of the last year had totally flipped his life upside down, and he had felt listlessly detached ever since, just going through the motions as a spectator to his own existence. The fallout from the lethal confrontation with the ATF last June had been quickly minimized by what had nearly turned into an all-out war with China. China continued to disavow the aerial action taken over the North Pacific, maintaining that it was carried out by some rogue element and that the Chinese Communist Party wished only for peace with the West. None of the leaders in Washington had the stomach for the material and economic damage that direct hostilities with China would cause, so they tacitly accepted the obvious fabrication. Once again, Weapons of Mass Destruction had preserved world peace.

On the home front, the struggle for water had not fully abated, but the violence committed in defense of Lake Superior ultimately did deter further attempts to action another cross-country pipeline. The response instead had been a significant uptick in population relocation, as citizens fled the dried-up

Southwestern deserts for the verdant Midwest and East Coast. The Michigan Militia's challenge to federal authority did not go unnoticed, although when federal prosecutors announced they would be seeking to charge all those involved in the protest-turned-firefight, the county and state level law enforcement branches both stated that they would resist any attempts by a federal agency to bring citizens into custody who they deemed to be lawfully protecting themselves from an aggressor.

Public sentiment in the region was clearly on the side of the protestors, and no arrests were made. This event signaled the beginning of a shift that had been building throughout the states for years. The creeping growth of power centralized within the federal government was finally being reined in. Months later, the ATF was quietly disbanded, heralding an era of shrinking federal reach.

None of this mattered much to Rob. Without his brother to labor alongside, he felt no motivation to continue his work in the iron mining industry. At the same time, he had little in the way of marketable skills outside of his rock-solid work ethic, but he was hoping that would be enough to carry him along. And that was why he was now pulling into a snow-covered parking space outside of a small office building with a sign reading "Michigan Aerospace Manufacturers Association" out front.

Rob had seen online that MAMA was recruiting for spaceborne construction workers. Piecing together information he had seen in the news, it looked like they were planning to utilize the Superior Launch Site to send machines, material, and people into Geostationary Orbit to build an orbital space station for the United States Space Force. The endeavor would require numerous launches to get the thousands of tons of equipment off the ground and launch sites across the country would be utilized together to fit the tight timelines. Today, he had his first interview for the position.

From what he gathered, the work itself would mostly involve operating robots and other machinery from a distance. That suited him just fine, as a lot of the work in the mines he had performed was of a similar nature. If he got the job, he would be required to be fully trained for Extra Vehicular Activity spacewalks, which gave him nervous jitters of excitement to think about. All in all, this seemed like just the opportunity he had been looking for. He could learn new skills, experience spaceflight, and put as much distance as possible between himself and his tragic past.

CHAPTER 20

Superior Launch Site, Michigan
May 1, 2032
0921 Hours EST

A cool bead of sweat trickled down Rob's neck as he sat strapped into the seat of a SpaceX Dragon 3 crew module. Although it was not at all warm inside the small passenger compartment, his nerves were running wild at the prospect of a real launch into space, causing him to perspire. Since taking the new job as a space construction operator just months ago, his life had turned into a fast-paced whirlwind of training and preparation. In the past, astronauts underwent years of training before ever leaving the Earth, but now the process had been condensed down to three months.

Rob stared straight ahead and tried to calm himself with slow, deep breaths while the two pilots ran through the pre-flight checklist. He had no role in this process, he and his three colleagues from the space-trained construction team were simply along for the ride. He was only half listening to the radio chatter over his headset, his mind drifting to the flight ahead.

Before he knew it, the final countdown began. He readied himself as the seconds were called out in the single digits. He felt a deep vibration as the main engine started up and began to burn off hydrogen, then the clock hit zero and the towering Falcon 9 rocket commenced the irreversible ignition process. The pilot's gloved finger actuated the ignition switch, sending an electrical signal at near lightspeed to the rocket engine computers, which then, working in tandem, executed the ignition routine across the array of nine engines.

The dual impeller turbopumps within each Merlin engine quickly spun up to a rotational rate of 36,000 revolutions per minute, forcing streams of liquid oxygen and rocket grade kerosene through the pintle injector and into the combustion chamber. There, the ensuing thermal reaction reached temperatures in excess of 5,000 degrees Fahrenheit, building up superheated gas at immense pressure which was forced out through the engine nozzle. The pressure of the gas generated by the set of engines imparted nearly two million pounds of lift to the vessel Rob was strapped into.

Rob felt the implacable force pressing him into his seat increasing as the rocket slowly began accelerating against gravity, upwards into the sky. Even through his headset, the throaty roar of the rocket engines was deafening, and he struggled to make out the radio chatter he was hearing. Over the next few minutes, the levels of force on his body oscillated as the engines cycled through different phases. He remained focused on the back of the pilot's head in front of him, resolving to pull through the trial of the launch.

Eventually the acceleration slackened, and the violent rumbling eased into a low vibration. Rob angled his head towards one of the heavily reinforced windows and his breath caught in his throat. A hazy blue and white curve stretched across the window against a backdrop of pure black. He realized he was seeing the Earth from beyond its atmospheric embrace. This was it. He was really in space.

CHAPTER 21

Peterson Space Force Base, Colorado
May 16, 2032
0957 Hours MST

Maria sat upright in a stiff-backed wooden chair situated in a small but well-lit waiting room. The two other chairs next to her stood empty, her only company being a distracted secretary engrossed in a dual-monitor computer display. She had been seated for ten minutes when the door ahead of her opened and a senior NCO wearing a crisply starched uniform strolled out, giving her a curt nod before striding briskly out of the waiting room.

The secretary spared a brief glance up from her computer to say, "Major Delgado, the general will see you now."

Maria stood up, pressed her shirt down with her open palms, then walked towards the door the NCO had exited from moments ago. The heavy oak door required a bit more effort than expected to push through, but the hinges were well oiled, and it silently eased open. She stepped inside and snapped a salute. Before her was a short, stocky man who appeared nearly as wide as he was tall, with broad shoulders that tugged at the seams of his immaculate uniform. Colored bars decorated his powerful chest, and despite his height he had a weighty presence that filled the room. A nametag adorning his right pectoral read "Ironwood."

"At ease, Major. Please have a seat," the general said.

Both officers took seats on opposite sides of a large brown desk, covered with neat piles of papers, pens, a laptop, tablet, and a handful of picture frames.

"Major Delgado," Ironwood began, "It's a pleasure to meet you in person. Your reputation certainly precedes you. I am honored by your service and sacrifice during the skirmish with China in 2030. But enough flattery. I've asked you here for a different reason."

Maria shifted uneasily in her seat. The praise made her uncomfortable, dredging up memories of fallen comrades. Fallen friends.

"As you're no doubt aware, we've reached a bit of a steady state in terms of the global balance of power. We walked right up to the brink of all out nuclear warfare, but a matched parity in hypersonic missile capabilities and anti-missile defenses looks like it will keep us out of a nuclear or direct conventional conflict for the time being. Within the bounds of Earth's atmosphere, that is. It's no secret that we've been working diligently to put tangible offensive and defensive assets in space for decades, and with construction of the orbital station underway, we are putting a plan in motion to develop both manned and unmanned combat-capable spacecraft. Ground-based R&D teams have been working on the project for years now, and our aim is to begin extraterrestrial flight tests as soon as the station is completed. I want you to lead the testing wings."

Ironwood paused to allow his words to sink in. Maria had no immediate response so the general continued.

"I've put in a transfer request to have you officially moved from the Air Force to the Space Force. You'll still be under the DAF of course and this transfer will come with a promotion to Lieutenant Colonel. You will undergo a six-month training cycle here at Peterson to prepare you for spaceflight and operations, then you and your team will be stationed in Geostationary Orbit conducting spaceflight tests. So, what do you say?"

Maria remained quiet for a few more seconds, mulling over the implications of what Ironwood had said. Then she replied, "Sir, it would be my pleasure to serve in that capacity. I accept."

"Well now, I'm glad to hear your enthusiasm. Do take a day or two to think it over as this will be a big commitment, but after you read through the transfer papers if you're still on board we'll get started right away."

"Thank you, sir. Will do."

"You are dismissed, Major."

With that, Maria stood, snapped a salute, then turned to make her exit.

As she marched down the hallway towards the door leading to the parking lot where her government-furnished rental car was waiting, her thoughts spun with the possibilities of what the future held. She would be going into space! While it had never been her personal end goal, it was undeniable that many Air Force test pilots aspired to one day join the astronaut corp. Granted, in the past decade, the number of individuals cleared to leave the Earth's atmosphere had increased dramatically, and the qualifications required to do so had proportionally decreased, but it was still a minuscule number relative to the population at large.

Her mind soon wandered to the dynamic of spaceflight itself. How would a craft handle in the absence of gravity or air resistance? More importantly, how would combat between spacecraft play out? She ultimately decided it would be impossible to predict without real time in the cockpit, and until that time came, she had much preparation to do.

CHAPTER 22

Alan Shepard Space Station, Geostationary Orbit
January 3, 2033
0758 Hours CST

After months of ceaseless labor from multiple shifts working around the clock, the first phase of construction of Alan Shepard Space Station had been completed. Rob had frankly been amazed at the level of planning and speed of execution. Thousands of tons of material had been lifted into geostationary orbit along with dozens of laborers and technicians. A prefabricated habitat module had been positioned and ready to go for the teams to stay in as soon as they arrived. Working in zero gravity had taken some getting used to, but after weeks of exposure he had adjusted well. Now that the station was built out, its spinning main body had Earth-like gravity generated from the centrifugal inertial force of the rotation. Walking the narrow corridors under the artificial centrifugal gravity he felt almost sluggish.

The cylindrical station was enormous, with a radius of almost one kilometer. A spinning layer of living quarters, offices, activity areas, and all other amenities coated the cylinder, protected by an outer shell of advanced radiation shielding. Extensive solar panel arrays poked out of either end like awkward wings. Remaining stationary in the center was the large zero-gravity shipyard, where new generations of spacecraft would be assembled. As it was still very much a militarized asset, an array of sensors and defensive satellites clouded around the station. Rob had heard that the Chinese were undertaking a similar effort to place a military installation in space with support from Russia, neither country wanting to give the United States an unchecked advantage in space.

The Shepard station was locked in orbit over 20,000 miles above the western hemisphere, always with a direct line of sight to ground-based sensor arrays within the United States. Its great distance from planet Earth meant that the "days" were considerably lengthier, since the sun was not blocked nearly as much, but the station still ran on Earth based timekeeping. This morning, Rob was headed to a meeting with the station chief, a man by the name of Forrestal. For what reason, he had not been made aware. As he made his approach to Forrestal's office, he was a little nervous. He knew he hadn't done anything wrong, at least nothing egregious, so it shouldn't be an appointment for disciplinary action.

The inside of the chief's office was filled only with the basic essentials, devoid of any trimmings. A desk held a computer with multiple monitors, straddled by a pair of chairs. The textured white walls matched the rest of the station's interior. A live plant in the corner added a modicum of character to the small cube, which also had a dinner-plate sized window offering an awe-inspiring view of Earth set against the starry blackness of outer space.

"Robert Ranta," Forrestal began, a statement more than a question. "I'll get right to it. One of the more critical endeavors we intend to use this station for is the mining of precious metals from asteroids. You have experience with modern mining practices. Is that correct?"

"Uh, yes, sir. Over a decade," Rob replied.

"Excellent. How would you like to stick around up here on the station and help form our mining team?"

"Well, I don't really know much about mining in space, or asteroids, or stuff besides copper and iron…"

Forrestal cut him off. "Ah don't worry, it's all similar enough. We'll be sending out rockets to pull an asteroid off its course when its path crosses close to Earth. As a matter of fact, we're tracking one that will be within an appropriate range in four months, hence why we're in a bit of a time crunch here. Once we have it matched to our orbit here at the station, we'll get the drilling machines and whatnot going. Well, you know better than I do how that all works. So, what do you say?"

Rob didn't have to think long. He didn't have any real plans for what he would do when he got back to Earth, and this seemed like it could be another interesting branch on his life path, so why not?

"I'm in," Rob responded, then added, "Sir."

CHAPTER 23

Alan Shepard Space Station, Geostationary Orbit
April 15, 2033
0700 Hours CST

Adjusting to life on Shepard Station had been an interesting transition for Maria. In many ways it just felt like living on a ship, something she had experienced multiple times during rescue and recovery exercises in the ocean. The sterile white hallways were alive with activity at all hours. The station was home to not only pilots, but all the other personnel one would expect on a standard military base, and an additional set of engineers and fabricator personnel working in the zero-gravity ship construction yard.

To avoid engineering complications, the Space Force was focusing on creating spacecraft that would never operate within Earth's atmosphere. The craft were built and launched already in space, and thus no consideration need be given to air drag, gravity, or the stress of atmospheric departure and re-entry. Maria had already flown a couple prototype designs, and while the internal cockpit layout largely matched that of the fighter jets she'd flown on earth, the experience of flying in space was vastly different. For one thing, the entire idea of the individual air-superiority fighter jet as she had known it on Earth had been largely tossed aside.

The development teams had come to an agreement that the drastically higher speeds that spacecraft could reach relative to their atmospherically bound cousins all but ruled out the possibility of traditional dogfighting. Instead, they were focused on waging a battle of technology, fought with information, extremely long range missiles, and countermeasures. In a way it was the next step in the evolution of BVR combat between Earth fighters. On top of that, there were many engineering limitations that could be lifted by removing the human pilot, even more so than on Earth. In that vein, the spacecraft combat structure relied to a great extent on fleets of hyper-specialized unmanned drones accompanied by a human-crewed command and control carrier.

Despite all that, a few billion dollars had still been allocated towards developing a manned space fighter, just in case. For that, Maria was grateful. The SF-12 Supernova was an absolutely beautiful machine; sleek, elegant, yet absurdly powerful. Its fuselage was quite similar to that of the F-25 Storm Crows she had been flying on Earth, with a classic stealth fighter profile, but the turbofan jet engine was replaced with a liquid fuel rocket engine. It also lacked traditional wings, which would provide little utility in the vacuum of space, although it did have two wing-like appendages. These "wings" held multidirectional compressed-gas maneuvering thrusters at their tips, giving them leverage over the fuselage so that they could reposition the craft more rapidly when fired.

Flying the craft was like nothing she had ever done within the bounds of Earth's atmosphere. Within minutes she could accelerate to a velocity of over 10,000 miles per hour, although in the emptiness of space it was almost impossible to tell how fast she was traveling without her onboard instruments. She could spin her craft 360 degrees in any direction in a split second, allowing her to face a target at any location in the three-dimensional space around her head-on, regardless of her relative direction of travel.

And of course, the onboard arsenal delighted her. The Supernova could hold twelve of the AIM-360 Joint Advanced Tactical Missiles, an updated version of the current air-to-air missile that was specialized for space operations and had a nearly infinite range, limited only by how often it had to maneuver directionally to track a target. Additionally, the fighter carried a complement of sixteen smaller RIM-200 Interceptor defensive missiles, which were designed to track and destroy incoming hostile missiles. The Interceptors carried less fuel and a smaller payload but could accelerate quickly to seek out and prematurely detonate a larger anti-ship missile. In theory, a RIM-200 could be used in an anti-ship capacity, but with the limited fuel reserve it wouldn't be able to adjust course enough to track over longer distances.

At the insistence of the pilot feedback team, a modified Vulcan rotary cannon was seated in the nose of the craft, lined up precisely with the spacecraft's center of gravity so that recoil would not substantially alter its trajectory. The gun was declared impractical by many on the development team, requiring a liquid cooling system as the cumulative heat of continuous firing would not efficiently dissipate within a vacuum. Yet the test pilots argued that there was no way to know what may or may not be a critical element of combat in space without tangible testing.

Intelligence was limited on what the Chinese and Russians were cooking up in the way of their own combat-capable spacecraft. She knew the Chinese now had a space station of their own in a geostationary orbit over the opposing hemisphere, and both sides were actively spying on the other through the vast networks of satellites and probes, but without human intelligence it was difficult to discern exact technical specifications and capabilities.

If neither side was willing to engage in open conflict on Earth, it seemed unlikely to Maria that they would fight within the relatively close (in astronomical terms) orbits they were in now either, where activity could be monitored just as closely as Earth's global airspace. Out past lunar orbit however, an object the size of a spacecraft, especially one built intentionally for stealth, would be almost impossible to detect or track. What might take place in the distant blackness beyond the moon was anyone's guess.

CHAPTER 24

Medium Earth Orbit
April 20, 2033
1730 Hours CST

Kenneth Hyde gazed out the round porthole window at the endless celestial ocean of stars. The shuttle ride to Shepard Station had given him plenty of time to reflect on his new assignment. In a way it felt like a demotion, being pulled from the high-threat top level missions with the SEAL teams to run a security detail on the new space station, but he grasped the importance of the new tasking. This station was pivotal to the continued global dominance of the United States, a key asset for force projection and protection of the military power and nuclear strike capabilities positioned in orbit. Almost more importantly though, it provided a path towards removing the reliance of foreign-held natural resources.

From consumer products to military hardware, the demand for rare metals was increasing exponentially with the continued integration of computer technology into all aspects of life. If the United States could access the metals held inside asteroids flying through the solar system on a regular basis, they could secure a practically limitless source of gold, silver, platinum, palladium, and many other valuable and crucial elements.

Given this high level of tactical and strategic value, it made sense that the Space Force would want only the best of the best to protect it. Kenneth also had a feeling that the Department of Defense was working towards establishing small-arms space combat doctrine. The first step on that path was to get warriors like himself operating in space in whatever capacity they could, then begin growing a program from there.

As a Navy SEAL, Kenneth was perfectly suited to the type of confined ship-board fighting that he expected would be the primary engagement environment of any combat involving foot soldiers. The SEAL teams were second to none when it came to maritime boarding actions, and he could already see many parallels between naval units on Earth's oceans, and military assets in space. One key difference however lay in the type of armaments that would be in use.

While it wasn't anticipated that firearms would be discharged onboard the space station, no sensible military advisor could rule it out. The walls of the station weren't fragile by any means, but a high velocity armor piercing bullet could cause serious problems, either from fully penetrating and exposing an open channel between the pressurized interior and the vacuum of space, or by damaging any of the various tubes and wires carrying electricity and vital gasses and fluids throughout the structure.

To account for that, he and his team were only issued weapons firing lower velocity .45 ACP frangible rounds, which would certainly still stop a person in their tracks if they took a hit but would lack real penetration power. Long term plans called for eventually reinforcing the external station walls, but it had already been a logistical nightmare getting the tons of structurally critical material into orbit, and the amount of heavy metal required to beef up station walls would be prohibitively expensive.

Under the assumption that any enemy force within the confines of a habitable space structure would be following a similar protocol, they would be eschewing their robust ceramic armor plates for lighter full body Kevlar armor systems that wouldn't stop high powered rounds but provided much more body surface coverage. Kenneth had also heard that there would be a stack of heavy ballistic shields in the station's armory.

Kenneth, like many other SEALs, preferred to move fast and light on any battlefield, but he recognized the shift in dynamic this new theater of war would bring. He knew that he and his men could adapt to all styles of combat and would be prepared to address any threat that may arise.

CHAPTER 25

Alan Shepard Space Station, Geostationary Orbit
May 5, 2033
1221 Hours CST

Rob was standing near the back of the tactical operations center, or TOC, observing the mission control process as a series of unmanned rocket-bearing vessels closed in on their asteroid target. The fleet of four ships carrying a collection of robotic components had been in flight for over sixteen hours, following a partial Hohmann transfer and utilizing the gravity well of the moon to reach the asteroid being tracked over 300,000 miles beyond the station. It wasn't the fastest or most direct approach, but it was the least fuel intensive path. Even this far out, the Earth's gravitational pull was still an omnipresent, albeit diminished, force that the ships had to work against to make headway out towards the asteroid.

The four ships consisted mostly of clustered rocket engines, fuel tanks, and a series of robotic arms and drills. The premise was straightforward: fly out to the asteroid, match orbit, position the drills, dig in, then fire the rockets to redirect the asteroid into the same geostationary orbit as Shepard Station, where it would be slowly positioned in proximity to the station for mining operations. The execution was vastly more complicated.

To begin with, the trajectory calculations to reach the asteroid had to be meticulously checked and rechecked, as small errors could result in total mission failure. That was the easy part, handled mostly by computers. What could not be predicted ahead of time was exactly what force vectors would need to be applied to the asteroid to bring it to the desired new orbit, since it was impossible to model the exact surface structure and center of mass of the small, distant object.

The asteroid, designated (277810) 2006FV35, was roughly the size of a football field and was estimated to weigh nearly one million tons. Fortunately, the rockets wouldn't need to apply too much force to guide the titanic mass of rock and metal back to the station. They would just tweak the asteroid's path enough to redirect it, allowing its existing momentum and Earth's own gravitational pull to slowly bring it to the desired orbit.

Once the ships made contact with the asteroid, they would arrange in such a manner to be able to vector the force of the combustion rockets in any direction to ensure full control over the adjustment of the asteroid's orbit. Unfortunately, due to the vast distance between the asteroid and the station, any radio signal inputs sent back and forth between the onboard computers controlling the rocket engines and robotic apparatuses and the TOC would take almost two seconds at peak separation. The shipboard computers should be capable of handling the trajectory calculations independently, but this meant there would be a non-negligible lag time for manual rocket thrust adjustments. Ultimately, for the first phase of the return trip, the asteroid just needed to travel in the general direction of the station, and as the distance decreased, finer adjustments could be made to steer it more precisely.

An array of small cameras and other onboard sensors was transmitting a lightspeed-lagged real-time view of what would be taking place, and everyone gathered in the TOC was focused on these feeds as the ships made their final approach to land on the asteroid. There wasn't a whole lot the assembled team could do at this stage besides watch and trust in the machinery and its programming. The hardware had been tested and the actions rigorously simulated beforehand, which paid off as the four ships made positive contact with the asteroid and began burning their engines to affect its orbit.

There were a few quiet cheers around the TOC, but the job was far from over so a full celebration would be premature. It would take days for the asteroid to make its way to Shepard Station. With that in mind, Rob departed to his quarters for some much-needed rest.

CHAPTER 26

Alan Shepard Space Station, Geostationary Orbit
May 5, 2033
1915 Hours CST

Specialist Jacobson was on duty in the Shepard Station traffic control center, validating incoming and outgoing shuttle flights. For the most part it was a fairly boring and prosaic duty, as there were usually only one or two arrivals or departures each day, so he had found ways to entertain himself and fill the time. One such pastime was to track the trajectories of the various craft on their orbits to and from Earth, his computer interface allowing him to delve into a deep collection of mundane details about any given flight.

He twisted back and forth in his lightly padded swivel chair, lazily scanning the monitors before him. Flight 67B was due in three hours, the only arrival for the day. He cycled through information panels and noticed that 67B was actually a few minutes behind schedule. Short delays like that were rare for space flights. Either the shuttles launched on time, or not at all. Perusing the flight history, he noticed a minor deviation had been made after the shuttle reached Low Earth Orbit, which was then quickly corrected, accounting for the delay. An interesting tidbit, but an event of little significance to Jacobson. He stared at the flight path a while longer, then turned his attention to other logfiles to pass the time.

CHAPTER 27

Alan Shepard Space Station, Geostationary Orbit
May 5, 2033
2042 Hours CST

Rob was getting ready for bed in his paltry bunk room when he got an alert on his station pager from one of the mining project supervisors: *Come to TOC now if awake.* With a sigh he slipped his shoes back on, slid open the thin polymer composite door, and sauntered off in the direction of the TOC.

When he arrived, he found the TOC abuzz with activity, a frantic tension in the air.

Rob sought out his supervisor and asked, "What's going on?"

"We lost contact with all of the rockets about an hour ago. We've been working to reestablish a link, but it now looks like the asteroid has altered course. It's not much but our projections show it's no longer on the path we had locked in at the time the rockets went dark."

Rob pondered this development, his ears picking up an animated exchange from a group of officers near the main displays.

"The rockets have gone rogue!"

"Impossible, there's no artificial intelligence onboard..."

"Some kind of glitch related to the loss of contact?"

"How do we know that the trajectory is off? At this distance can we really be sure?"

"The calculations are elementary. We've confirmed them on multiple systems."

The mission commander, a man Rob knew as Colonel Miller, interjected, his strident voice cutting through the hubbub.

"We must assume that control of the rockets has been seized by an outside entity. Assemble a flight team and prep our combat squadrons for an immediate launch. We're going to get eyes on the rock and figure out exactly what's going on out there."

This declaration was met with a series of "yes, sir's", and his staff sprang into action.

Five minutes later, a troupe of pilots already dressed in flight suits filed into the TOC for a briefing on the situation. Rob's eyes lingered on the woman leading the line of pilots. She was the shortest of the bunch, but her serious demeanor exuded confident authority. She had close cropped brown hair and dark Latin-American features. Even in the unflattering flight suit he found her startlingly attractive.

Rob quickly brought his focus back to the status of the asteroid mission and the orders being belted out by Colonel Miller.

"Expect a thirty-six-hour mission. I want you on a fast intercept course for that asteroid. We don't know what's out there but assume an enemy force with hostile intent. We have confirmed we have no assets out that far, so you are cleared to engage any and all spacecraft on sight. Dismissed."

The pilots emptied out of the TOC, no doubt heading for the shuttle hangar. Rob knew that the Space Force had spent astronomical amounts of money and labor hours developing combat spacecraft, but as far as he was aware they had not yet encountered any practical use applications. It seemed as if that was about to change. Perhaps the future of space warfare had finally arrived.

CHAPTER 28

100,000 miles from Earth
May 5, 2033
2200 Hours CST

Maria was settled into the cockpit of her Supernova for a long flight. She was accompanied by one other Supernova, and a pair of SC-2 Perseid drone carriers. The carrier ships were controlled by a three-person human crew, and each held a complement of six supermaneuverable SQ-14 Gamma drone fighters.

The Gamma fighters were compact craft, eschewing space for a human pilot and life support systems in exchange for a small supercomputer that allowed the drone craft to initiate and respond to combat actions. The drone fighters still had an elongated fuselage that allowed them to minimize their profile as seen from two of the three spatial dimension planes, with a main rocket engine mounted in the rear and additional thrusters facing other directions. They were essentially just mobile, intelligent missile platforms, but they still relied on signals from a human onboard the carrier for overall tactical direction.

As for Maria's own craft, she was confined to the cramped cockpit for the duration of the mission. She had run simulator training exercises where she had spent up to forty-eight consecutive hours in the flight seat, urinating into a diaper and consuming liquid nutrients from a tube, but no amount of training could lessen the discomfort. She had just adapted to dealing with it, pushing physical botherations from her mind and directing her attention to the mission at hand.

Her small force had burned hard to push farther and farther from Earth's grasp, having just detached from sets of booster rockets after reaching a speed of nearly 50,000 miles per hour. Now the faint tug of Earth's gravity began to gradually decelerate them as they cruised towards their target.

Maria still wasn't seeing any objects of significance on her scanners aside from the tracked asteroid, but she assumed any hostile craft would be designed for stealth just as hers was. It occurred to her that she was now a greater distance from her home planet than she had ever been in her life. She knew some of her fellow pilots must be nervous about the potential to encounter a real combat scenario in the new frontier of space, but not her. Maria was keyed up and ready to go, just itching to put her billion-dollar spaceship to work doing what it was made for. As James would have said, her fangs were out.

CHAPTER 29

153,000 miles from Earth
May 6, 2033
0010 Hours CST

"I got something."

One of the pilots from the Perseid designated Venus Three broke what had been a long silence with news of a sensor contact. Maria rechecked her own computer and saw the contact information that had been shared across her squadron.

"Venus One confirming. Looks like a group of five or six individual objects shadowing the asteroid," Maria responded.

The combination of radar and optical scanning had picked up what Maria assumed must be enemy craft at a distance of about 5,000 miles. Maria and her wingmates had been consistently decelerating over the past couple hours but their velocity away from Earth was still in excess of 15,000 miles per hour. At their current angle of approach, they would intercept the asteroid in fifteen minutes, then go careening past. She wanted to maintain a high velocity to engage the potential enemy spacecraft, but eventually she would need to match trajectories with the asteroid.

"All Venus elements, initiate 5,000 knot deceleration and adjust heading by two zero degrees," Maria ordered.

She engaged her wing thrusters to spin her craft around nearly 180 degrees, then fired her rear-mounted rocket engine for a couple minutes to bleed off speed and impart a minor lateral acceleration. The other craft in her command followed suit. Maria continued to monitor her computer display, which kept tabs on the enemy locations even while she was physically facing away from them.

"Hostile contacts are adjusting trajectory. Looks like they're breaking off from the asteroid," called out a crew member on one of the Perseids.

Maria's response came quickly.

"Venus Two, cut deceleration. Venus Three and Four, deploy drones. We should have missile locks in sixty seconds. Weapons free."

The carriers would hang back while Maria, her wingman, and two full drone squadrons would continue on to engage.

"Venus Three, Gammas out."

"Venus Four, Gammas out."

"Heads up, now tracking sixteen bogies. Spread out target locks. I want four missiles on each. Fire when ready."

Maria had to assume the enemy vessels were running multiple anti-missile countermeasures, the same as her own, so the prevailing tactic was to overload them with a high enough volume of offensive missiles so as to slip some through any defenses. Her last command was met with a round of affirmation from her team. Maria cycled through her targeting computer to line up her own missile locks and prepared to fire. She assumed the opposing force must have been running their own type of carrier craft, and most likely deployed squadrons of supporting drones. It was no surprise to her. Despite the United States developing their technology in the utmost secrecy, general design principles always seemed to find their way to the Chinese somehow, and Maria had no doubt that the craft arrayed against her were Chinese.

The missile lock tone sounded in her ear, and she depressed the firing studs to send four of her twelve missile arsenal lancing out through the empty blackness towards the distant opposing force. The missiles blasted through the vacuum, accelerating rapidly, gaining thousands of miles per hour on top of the inherent velocity already imparted from traveling with their host ship. Simultaneously, a swarm of identical missiles was unleashed by her human wingman and the dozen drone fighters, blazing through the space ahead of her like a meteor shower before quickly fading out of sight.

At this point, Maria fully expected that a responding salvo of missiles had been fired by the enemy fleet, but the smaller objects wouldn't be detectable just yet. The cluster of friendly missiles continued accelerating for a full minute, eating up thousands of miles of distance while closing on their targets. In stark contrast to the dull hours leading up to the engagement, the pace of the battle suddenly accelerated as quickly as a JTAM as the opposing sides began exchanging missiles. Maria could barely keep up with the flurry of comms traffic while focusing on bringing down her enemies and keeping her own ship in one piece.

"Hostile missiles detected!"

"Keep Interceptors on automatic."

"Twelve bruisers down, no joy."

"Interceptors out."

"Scratch one bandit!"

"Gamma Six is KIA."

The activity had an eerie feel to it. While her communications headset was full of chatter, the rest of her senses lacked the stimulation to match it. Some information from her onboard computer was being holographically projected onto her cockpit canopy, but gazing out through the reinforced glass, the only true visual indication that she was in combat were brief, pinprick flashes of light representing far off missile explosions. Not currently under any acceleration, her ship felt completely still, as if she was just sitting in an office. Her radar-optical sensor display computer painted the most accurate picture of the engagement, which made it feel all the more like a simulator.

Despite thousands of pounds of explosives and hundreds of millions of taxpayer dollars being expended, only a couple fighters on each side had gone down. Meanwhile, the two forces were quickly approaching the merge. Maria's aim was for her fighters to eliminate all enemy ships escorting the asteroid before they reached it and subsequently went whizzing by with their substantial velocity, then they could burn off the fuel needed to return to the asteroid with minimal risk. To that end, she knew she needed to act decisively to eliminate the remaining enemy squadrons.

"All Gamma units fire six more missiles on network link then go independent," Maria ordered, adding two missiles of her own to the attack and hoping that an even larger wave of offensive missiles could overpower the enemy's tight defensive bubble.

Her command was relayed to the group of drones by their carrier crews, and a large volley of high explosive missile warheads took off towards the enemy ships. The distance had closed considerably, and the results of the missile launches came back much quicker. What also came back quickly at her fleet was a wall of hostile missiles. Maria couldn't expend her valuable attention tracking the full report of hits and misses, but fortunately one of the crew members monitoring the action from the rear onboard a Perseid carrier was able to keep her informed.

"I'm reading eleven confirmed kills, five active bandits. Based on the combat playback, I believe we're dealing with two carriers and three fighters," a female officer manning the tactical display calmly read out. Her life may not have been in immediate danger, but if her allied fighters were destroyed, the carrier she was flying in would stand no chance against even a single enemy fighter, so her life still very much depended on a victory. "Be advised all Gamma drones are KIA."

Maria considered the battle space. Assuming two of the remaining enemy ships were carriers, it was two against three, to her disadvantage. Now at a range of only a few hundred miles, her targeting computer was able to provide her more detailed profiles of the remaining enemy ships. Two of the craft were larger than the rest. Those must be the carriers. There was also a pair of much smaller fighters, while the last ship was in between the two. Based on this information, Maria now gathered that of the three hostile fighters, two were drones and only one was piloted by a human. While Maria firmly believed that no AI was yet on the level of the most skilled human pilots, she knew man and machine were nearly at parity, so the odds were still in her opponent's favor.

She would now have to work with her wingman, a pilot whom she had never met before arriving in space and had never gone into battle with before, to outfly the enemy trio.

"Venus Two, missile count?"

"Three bruisers."

"Put one on each of the smaller ships and hold one back."

"Yes ma'am. Firing now."

Maria sent one missile of her own at each of the suspected drones, and another three at what had to be the lone human-piloted enemy fighter, leaving her with a single remaining offensive missile as well. She watched as one, then another of her missiles detonated well before reaching their targets.

"Good kill," Venus Two called out as she saw an icon marking an enemy drone wink out of existence on her targeting computer.

Maria continued staring at the paths of two of her missiles accelerating to intercept the hostile human pilot. One of them went dark but one more stayed on course. Maria held her breath as it appeared that the last missile was about to enter the kill zone. She stared out her canopy and saw a flash of light where a red icon indicated the position of the enemy fighter, but the red icon remained. Checking back with her main computer display, she confirmed the fighter was still flying.

"Aaaand another!" her wingman stated triumphantly.

Maria hesitated for a split second before realizing he had been referring to the other hostile drone. Between the two of them they now had only two offensive missiles left with which to engage the enemy fighter, and a handful of interceptors if it came to that. Maria suspected that the fighter that they continued to close with was saving its remaining missiles for close range shots which would be more difficult to counter. She wanted to take it out before it got that opportunity, but in all likelihood the enemy pilot had the countermeasures to dodge two more missiles, which would leave her and her wingman in a poor position. As her mind ran through scenarios, she realized she did have one weapon with no practical countermeasure.

Maria pulled up the holographic reticle display for her Vulcan cannon and assigned a full lock on the enemy fighter. Just as it had in her old Raptor or Storm Crow, once locked on, the targeting computer would calculate a firing solution in real time that would match the ballistic trajectory of the cannon to the flight path of the enemy craft. Now, these calculations, which were being updated sixty times per second, were adjusted to the physics of the vacuum.

At the ranges they had been fighting before, these firing solutions were all but useless. The level of precision needed to land an unguided 20mm projectile on a target area of just a few square yards at a range of over a thousand miles was so high that her craft didn't even possess the granularity of movement and positioning required to accurately aim the weapon at such a target. An adjustment of a single millimeter could change the impact point by the length of a football field at that range, not to mention if the target accelerated in any capacity during the long travel time of the projectile, it would completely nullify the targeting trajectory of any rounds in flight.

Now she was only a few hundred miles from her target. The odds were still long but the shot was not infeasible. Maria engaged the cannon auto-lock and felt her ship budge slightly as the flight computer made micro-maneuvers with her wing-mounted thrusters to line the gun up with the trajectory calculated to score a hit. Without hesitating, Maria briefly tapped the trigger for the Vulcan cannon, firing a short burst of about fifty armor-piercing rounds. Given that she was aiming at an angle off of her exact direction of travel, she knew that the reaction impulse from the compressed gas expelling the first group of large bullets through the cycling barrels of the cannon would impart an opposing force on her ship that the flight computer would struggle to compensate for in real time, rendering any sustained fire woefully inaccurate.

"Guns, guns, guns," she spoke aloud with little conviction.

Maria paused, allowing the targeting system to realign her ship, then fire again. She repeated this process two more times, hoping to increase her odds of a hit. The cannon rounds departed from her ship at a velocity of over 2,000 miles per hour. Adding in the speed of the ship they had been fired from brought the rounds up to around 12,000 miles per hour. On top of that, the target fighter was moving towards the incoming rounds with a directional velocity of another 4,000 miles per hour. Given the overall relative approach velocity, one of the half-pound 20mm x 167mm depleted-uranium armor piercing rounds would impact with a kinetic energy of over 28 million joules, were it to make contact with the enemy ship. The enemy pilot had no way of detecting the small, lethal projectiles hurtling towards his spacecraft.

While Maria waited for her bursts of cannon fire to reach their target, she thought she could just barely make out the visual outline of her opponent now. She also saw a series of faint flares and immediately heard the warning chime of multiple missile launch detections. It looked like the enemy pilot had decided he was now close enough and had unloaded with what was probably all five of his remaining missiles.

"Incoming!" She called out to her wingman.

"I got three on me, last of my Interceptors going out!" he exclaimed in reply.

Maria still had eight of the defensive Interceptor missiles, so she released six of them, doubling up on some of the incoming missiles. Seconds later she felt her gut clench with dread as one of the incoming missiles blazed past an Interceptor, heading right at her. It was too late to launch another Interceptor with any hope of catching it, so she triggered her wing thrusters to turn her heading ninety degrees from the missile, waited until she was nearly inside its kill zone, then blasted her rocket engine at full thrust and simultaneously dumped a thick cloud of chaff. Maria figured she had a window of about one tenth of a second to pull off the dodge. If she accelerated too early, the missile would be able to react and catch her on a new intercept course. If she started too late, the missile would get close enough to her to detonate and catch her in the blast, either outright destroying her ship or leaving it so crippled she would be effectively dead.

Just as Maria's engine was lighting off, a brief set of radio transmissions barely registered in her ears.

"I can't, I, ah-"

"Venus Two is down, Venus Two is down!"

Maria realized her wingman had just been taken out but she had no room to dwell on that fact as her full attention was on her own situation. She was suddenly pressed back into her seat with the force of ten Gs, quite nearly blacking out from the instant change exerted on her body in spite of her G-suit and extensive physical training. The hostile missile flew past her fighter, ignoring the inert chaff as well. The missile had passed her at a speed of 20,000 miles per hour and was already miles away before it began arcing around to come at her again. As the missile's relative velocity slowed, Maria fired off one more Interceptor, which easily caught and destroyed the missile.

During this exchange, the opposing pilot had seen no need to burn fuel on any unnecessary acceleration, and as such was still moving along the same path as when Maria had fired her cannon at it. This tactically sensible decision would prove to be his downfall. The enemy pilot was probably still unaware of the hundred or so cannon rounds zipping past the vicinity of his fighter, and certainly had no time to become aware of his situation once one lucky round struck the fuselage of his ship.

As the small, dense cannon shell impacted the sleek alloy frame of the space fighter, millions of joules of energy were transferred to the metallic structure. The depleted-uranium shell punched through layers of metal and plastic before passing completely through the ship, deformed, wobbling, and possessing significantly less speed. The energy it left behind to be absorbed by the ship's structure excited the molecules of the spaceship's frame into an unstable state, breaking down the tight lattices of the metal alloy and causing the ship to disintegrate. Nearly instantaneously, heat-energy from the atomized structure reached the rocket fuel supply, igniting the kerosene-based propellant.

Maria, having just stabilized her ship in the wake of her evasion of the tenacious missile, turned her craft to face her opponent again just in time to witness the spectacular fireball of his destruction.

"Alpha Mike Foxtrot," she muttered.

CHAPTER 30

Alan Shepard Space Station, Geostationary Orbit
May 6, 2033
0030 Hours CST

Technical Sergeant Melissa Wilson was watching over the array of monitors in the Base Defense Operations Center, a posting that had been largely uneventful. She was excited to have gotten a chance to go up into space. It was the main reason she had enlisted in the Space Force after all, but now having spent months onboard Shepard Station, the novelty of life in space had worn off.

Her attention was now directed towards the main personnel docking bay, where transport flight 67B was preparing to offload a team of contracted service staff and a haul of basic supplies. So far it was another routine docking. All the clearance codes checked out. Melissa observed the airlock camera feed, seeing a pair of men wearing flight helmets with dark tinted visors covering their faces. They looked like pilots. Normally the passengers would debark first, but it was possible they were all busy preparing the cargo for unloading.

The military police guard stationed at the airlock door confirmed the pressure in the airlock chamber was equalized, then keyed the sliding door open. One of the helmeted figures stepped through into the receiving hallway. The guard began making a motion to greet the new arrival, when suddenly the faceless individual whipped a compact pistol out of a deep pocket in the flight suit and fired a single shot into the guard's head. The MP dropped to the floor in a motionless heap.

Heavily armored figures bearing thick ballistic shields and short barreled firearms began pouring through the airlock, moving quickly down the corridor and firing on any station personnel they encountered.

Melissa stared frozen with shock for a split second until her training took over.

"Lock down sector two, now!" she snapped at a security officer manning a control console.

At her command, powered doors throughout the station designed to compartmentalize the structure in case of emergency slid shut and locked. Next, Melissa pressed a button on her personal tablet computer to page all security forces on the station to kit up and prepare for imminent defensive action. She then called up the station security force leader Kenneth Hyde.

"Commander Hyde."

His response came hastily.

"Sergeant Wilson."

"At least twenty heavily armed and armored hostiles have breached the airlock on deck two. They're currently in section Bravo Three. I'm not sure how long the emergency doors will hold them. Get your teams fully geared up and over to Bravo Four ASAP. I'll keep you updated on enemy movements.

"Hard copy, Sergeant. Moving now."

Melissa turned back to her team in the BDOC.

"Smith, remote release that ship and override the airlock seal. I want Bravo Two and Three fully vented."

"On it, ma'am."

Melissa hoped she could end the incursion right here and now before more friendly blood was shed. Her hopes were dashed when Specialist Smith reported back seconds later.

"Ma'am, those doors aren't responding. They must be jammed or there's some sort of local hack."

Another officer in the BDOC raised her voice for Melissa's attention.

"Ma'am, look at feed five. They're opening the door to Bravo Four!"

It appeared that the boarders had some sort of technical equipment allowing them to override the electronic locking mechanism, and a door that should have been locked down slid open, allowing the hostile force to pass into the next section of the station. Melissa's thoughts were racing, and she reacted right away.

"Cut power to the emergency door to Bravo Five."

"Yes, ma'am."

Melissa continued watching as the invaders approached the next door and brought out their equipment again, this time to no effect. *This should keep them penned in at least while Commander Hyde's teams got into position*, Melissa thought. Moments later one of the hostile gunmen produced what appeared to be a high-powered cutting torch and began burning through the outline of the emergency door.

"Fuck."

Melissa spat the curse out, racking her brain for ways to hold the invaders at bay.

CHAPTER 31

153,000 miles from Earth
May 6, 2033
0032 Hours CST

Upon seeing their entire fighter complement taken out, the two enemy carrier ships broke off from the asteroid and made to leave the area. Maria spun her craft and initiated a hard lateral burn to arc her trajectory towards them. She considered firing her last AIM-360 at one of the fleeing ships. She was even close enough that she could probably make the other kill with the final Interceptor as well. While the enemy carriers showed no signs of offensive missile capabilities, they could still very well possess some anti-missile defenses though, and it would be imprudent to waste her only remaining missiles on relatively easy targets.

"Venus Three and Four, rendezvous with the asteroid. I'll chase down these squirters," Maria said to her fellow pilots.

After scoring an admittedly lucky guns kill, Maria figured it was time to utilize the Vulcan cannon in the manner she had originally envisioned when she stubbornly pushed back against the R&D engineers who were trying to get rid of it. Maria's smaller Supernova fighter had much less mass than the bulky enemy carriers, which allowed her to accelerate at a substantially higher rate. The carriers appeared to be firing their engines at full thrust, but fifteen minutes later she was settling in behind the two ships, slowly closing the final miles between them.

Since the enemy ships were continuing to accelerate,

Maria knew she would need to be relatively close to land her shots. The fleeing vessels attempted a course change, splitting off in opposite directions. Maria chose one to tail, deciding she would track the next one down afterwards. She was mindful of her fuel level, but now that her velocity was vectored towards the general direction of Earth, and therefore Shepard Station, she wouldn't need too much more for the return journey.

Maria closed to a distance of just a few miles behind the ship she was following. The burning tail-mounted rocket engine was shining as bright as a second sun before her, which also presented an easy visual target. Not that she needed one with the assistance of her advanced targeting computer, but it felt good to boresight an enemy with her own two eyes. When she was ready to fire, Maria drastically throttled up the thrust from her engine so that her craft was traveling with significantly more velocity than the enemy ahead of her. Right before she squeezed the trigger, she cut thrust completely so that she wouldn't overtake her own cannon rounds. She gave the trigger a long pull, letting off a stream of about one hundred armor-piercing shells, then quickly pulled up on her flight stick, causing a jet of compressed gas to be expelled from a small thruster under the nose of the craft, following the motion up with a short burst from her main rocket engine to break off the tail of the enemy ship.

Due to the extra relative velocity Maria had given her cannon shots at the time of firing, they caught up to their target in a matter of seconds. They didn't impact with nearly as much kinetic energy as her first kill, but dozens of destructive depleted-uranium rounds tore into the rear of the ship, gutting the vessel. Gallons of volatile rocket fuel leaked out and were ignited by the still-thrusting engine, causing an uncontrolled conflagration to envelop the perforated spaceship.

Maria immediately began maneuvering to track down the other enemy. A few minutes later she was angling towards the hapless carrier. Rather than falling in directly behind, she was approaching on a slightly less than perpendicular intercept path. For this shot, she relied on the computer to calculate an appropriate firing trajectory based on the constant acceleration of the target ship. Once her computer was holding her ship on a locked heading with a high probability of scoring a hit, she unleashed two solid bursts, taking her ammunition stores below 25% capacity.

Unlike her previous two victims, this last ship didn't explode after taking hits from the cannon. It was evident her rounds had had some effect though as the carrier lost all acceleration. Without any ability to change its now fixed vector, the wounded carrier was easy pickings. As Maria's trajectory took her past the drifting ship, her wing-mounted gas thrusters rotated her fighter, keeping her deadly Vulcan cannon aligned with the enemy vessel. At the perigee of her fly-by, she triggered another burst of cannon fire, raking the enemy with a torrent of hard hitting 20mm shells and ensuring that the ship was now dead in space.

The frenetic battle having at last concluded, Maria called out to the station.

"Venus One for Shepard Station."

Ten seconds passed with no response.

"Venus One for Shepard Station," she repeated.

Still nothing.

"Venus One for Shepard Station, do you read?"

"Venus One, this is Shepard Actual, sorry we, uh, have a bit of a situation over here," a familiar voice from the Tactical Operations Center came in over her headset. She detected a nervous tinge to the words.

"Are you still tracking us? We secured the asteroid, but we took heavy losses. We need to RTB now. Are you back in contact with the asteroid rockets?"

"Ah okay, yes. Yes, our connection is live again. Re-vectoring the asteroid now."

"Copy. Are we cleared to leave the rock and return to the station?"

"Um," the voice on the other end of the radio paused. "Yes,

clear to RTB."

"Shepard, what's going on back there?" Maria demanded.

"We've been boarded by a hostile force. Station security is engaging now. I- I think they can hold them off."

Maria was stunned into silence. The station was under attack? How? There was nothing she could do from her position deep into distant space. She figured by the time she reached the station hours from now, the invaders would either be repelled, or she would no longer have anywhere to dock. As she plotted a course for the lengthy return voyage, she contemplated the implications of the latter outcome.

CHAPTER 32

Alan Shepard Space Station, Geostationary Orbit
May 6, 2033
0034 Hours CST

In a matter of minutes, Kenneth had transitioned from relaxing down time to fully equipped and ready for battle. He met most of his team at the armory, where he donned a Kevlar armor suit that offered protection from small caliber non-armor piercing projectiles to his torso, neck, shoulders, groin, and thighs. He also put on a helmet with a thick transparent ballistic face shield that allegedly could stop most pistol rounds. His service pistol was already in a holster on his hip, a position it only left during PT sessions or when he was showering or sleeping. Moving briskly through the armory, he grabbed a compact SIG MPX submachine gun chambered for .45 ACP with a 4.5-inch barrel off the rack and filled the pouches on his vest with fully loaded magazines before grabbing one more magazine and slotting it into the magwell of the MPX. He fingered the bolt carrier release to lock a round into the chamber, then slipped the weapon's single point sling over his head.

Next, he picked up a Benelli M1014 semi-automatic 12-gauge shotgun with a shortened barrel and folded stock. He flipped the shotgun over and thumbed in five shells loaded with #4 Buckshot. The 6.1mm lead balls in the shells lacked the stopping power and penetration of the usual 00 Buckshot, but they could still be lethal up close, and the wider spread made firing the weapon very user-friendly. He racked a shell into the chamber, then slipped one more into the magazine tube and slung the weapon at his off-dominant side. Kenneth topped off his loadout with a bandolier of M84 flashbang grenades then began running towards the location of the enemy's breach. The gear weighed a considerable amount, but it was well distributed across his body. Besides, he'd spent weeks rucking sixty pounds of kit up the steep, rugged slopes of the Alborz range in Northern Iran. This was nothing.

On his way over he heard the voice of Melissa in his earpiece.

"Commander, the hostiles are in Bravo Four and are cutting the door to Bravo Five."

"Copy, we'll be at Bravo Five in thirty seconds."

"It looks like it will take them another minute at least. Be advised we count twenty-six combatants, most wearing full body armor and armed with submachine guns."

Kenneth had eleven other men with him. Well, nothing was ever easy. Kenneth and his team moved through empty corridors, all non-combat personnel having retreated deeper into the station. His team formed up outside the door to Bravo Five then cautiously made entry. He could see the sparking glow of an oxyacetylene cutting torch carving an outline around the borders of the door. It made for an odd standoff, each force braced and waiting for the door to come down and the bullets to start flying. Kenneth figured the boarders had foregone explosive breaching charges as they did not want to risk blowing out any walls keeping out the hard vacuum of space or damaging other critical station infrastructure. They wanted to take the station intact.

If Kenneth and his men had rifles with full metal jacketed ammunition, they would just open fire right now, perforating the door and the enemy combatants on the other side. As it was, their hollow-tipped subsonic Automatic Colt Pistol rounds would do little to break through the sturdy alloyed steel door, so they set up and waited for the enemy to make entry and expose themselves.

Kenneth had his security operators arrayed in a slight

arc at the back of the Bravo Five module where they could retreat through the next door if necessary. Six men were crouched in the front line, each propping up a heavy ballistic shield and wielding submachine guns single handed. Behind them, Kenneth and three other operators were arranged in low stances, weaving in lines of fire over the shoulders of the shield-bearers. The last two men were in cover on opposite sides of the open doorway. The position they held was about sixty feet from the enemy's breach point.

An ordinary man may have buckled under the nervous pressure of waiting for a gunbattle that could break out at any second, but all the soldiers under Kenneth's command came from elite fighting units and held their positions with hardened resolve. Kenneth's finger caressed the trigger of his shouldered .45 caliber MPX as he played the red dot of the rail-mounted holographic sight across the burning door. He ran through scenarios in his head of what the engagement would look like, and after thinking through his action plans, he reached to his vest with his left hand and slid out a flashbang grenade. He slid the safety pin out with his thumb, keeping his palm pressed against the strike lever.

Less than one minute passed, though it felt like one hundred, when the outline of the cut in the door appeared to be completed and the sparking ceased. *Here we go*. Kenneth felt his squadmates shifting around him, preparing for an imminent engagement. Without fanfare, the door fell forward and the air was immediately filled with bullets traveling up and down the corridor. Kenneth hurled his flashbang towards a wall of bulletproof shields and armored figures, the strike lever falling out as it left his hand, arming the grenade. Two objects, which had to be concussion grenades of some type, came flying from the other end of the hallway, not quite reaching his position.

Kenneth fired a burst of five rounds towards the enemy then ducked down and squeezed his eyes shut just before the pair of grenades before him detonated. His PELTOR headset took some of the edge off the 170-decibel explosion, but he was still momentarily deafened and left blinking away a stark white after image. He knew most of his men would be experiencing a similar level of disorientation, but the veteran warriors stayed in the fight. Some men fired blindly down the corridor while they recovered to maintain a high volume of fire, the mass of armored enemies leaving no shortage of targets.

Plenty of bullets from both sides were finding their marks, but with minimal effect. Kenneth had already felt the punch of multiple impacts against his armor carapace, but the frangible rounds were being halted or turned away before causing any critical damage. The heavy ballistic shields on both sides were taking the brunt of the assault. Kenneth knew that eventually enough bullet strikes would tear through any amount of infantry armor, although there were also still small sections of exposed flesh. He steadied his breathing, switched his fire selector to semi-automatic, and made a few precise shots. He was rewarded when an enemy soldier stumbled back from the formation. Unfortunately, no vital areas were exposed, so it was unlikely to be an incapacitating wound.

Kenneth heard grunts of pain as slicing bullets found their way around the armor coverage of his own men. The width of the corridor served to even the playing field, as there was not enough room for all of the enemy combatants to bring their weapons to bear, but as soon as one enemy went down, another was there to take his place, a luxury Kenneth's group did not possess. He snapped off an additional series of shots, then ducked down, thumbing the mag release button to drop out the dry magazine then slotting in a fresh one before the empty one hit the floor.

When Kenneth brought his weapon back up to the firing line, he noted that the enemy was slowly advancing down the hallway, an implacable armored phalanx that evoked visions of a Roman legionnaire formation. The floor around him was littered with spent magazines and shell casings, and the air was hazy with gun smoke. As his operators struggled to land meaningful shots against the opposing mass of soldiers, he suspected that this was going to devolve into a brutal melee.

The man in front of Kenneth went down, the location of the final blow that felled him unclear. Kenneth slid forward to grab the man's shield, keeping it upright and facing the enemy. He felt the pounding of bullets impacting the other side, thus far none succeeding in punching through. Melissa was in his ear, feeding him a live tactical overview from her security camera viewpoint.

"You have six men down. It looks like they've lost eight or nine. Enemy is halfway to your position."

As the enemy drew closer, the ferocity of the small arms fire increased, and Kenneth knew they would be ripped apart. They needed to regroup, so he reluctantly gave the order to retreat.

"Fall back!" he shouted into his microphone.

Immediately the remaining members of his team began backing through the door behind them, keeping ballistic shields raised and returning automatic gunfire. A man beside Kenneth fell to the floor, his right leg stitched with crimson blossoms, but the man kept moving, attempting to crawl through the exit. Kenneth let his weapon fall loose in its sling around his neck and grabbed the crawling man's drag handle, pulling him the rest of the way through the doorway while he kept the heavy shield up with his other hand.

As soon as Kenneth and his wounded teammate were through the door, the sliding metal slabs slammed shut on remote command from the BDOC. It killed Kenneth to leave fallen comrades behind, but under the withering barrage of bullets there was no choice. With a brief reprieve from the gunfire, he took stock of the situation. Surveying his surviving men, he saw that all were torn up from multiple bullet impacts, most of them bleeding from at least one location. They loaded in fresh magazines and ensured their equipment was ready for another round of combat.

There was no way Kenneth and his small team could defeat the numerically superior foe in the tight confines of the space station in any type of conventional fight, but he knew he absolutely could not fail in his mission to protect the station. The command staff would scuttle the station before allowing it to fall into enemy hands, but even so it would be almost impossible for the United States to recover from the blow to her efforts in the global power struggle. He heard muffled shots coming from the other side of the door and his heart tightened as he realized that it must be the enemy soldiers dead-checking the half of his team still on the other side with bullets to the head.

He considered falling back and engaging in guerilla tactics throughout the station. There were extra weapons in the armory to arm some of the station crew members as well. That wouldn't work out though. Not only would the odds of success still be low, but if the hostile force was allowed deeper into the station, they could cause immeasurable damage to the station itself even if the defenders proved difficult to ferret out. They must be stopped here.

An idea formed in his head, and he looked up to address his men. Meanwhile, the cutting torch had started up on the now unpowered door they had just retreated through.

"Jansen. Rogers. Stackowitz. Brown. O'Malley. I'm going to breach the wall and start venting these sectors. Then it'll become a matter of holding the enemy until we all suffocate. This will be a one-way mission, but I believe it's our only option for preserving the station. Any objections?"

No one spoke. Each man's face wore a mask of grim resolve. They had all faced death on multiple occasions before and had come to terms with their mortality long ago. Furthermore, they knew their duty and would not balk from doing what needed to be done to defend their country and their families that called it home.

Lieutenant Brown broke the silence.

"We're all in, sir."

"Melissa, seal the door to Bravo Six."

A deep thud signaled the closing of the door behind them.

"We'll need to buy as much time as possible. With our smaller number we'll have to fight them at the choke point of the doorway."

Kenneth and his men lined up on either side of the door that was currently being cut through and prepared for their counterassault. Each man held a flashbang grenade ready to toss. Kenneth drew his Benelli shotgun and chose a spot along the wall bordering the outside vacuum. When the cutting torch stopped, Kenneth pressed his shotgun to the wall and fired a single shell at point blank range. Without any distance to dissipate the concentrated energy of the shot, the 12-gauge load punched through the wall, opening a fist-sized leak to the vacuum on the other side. A low whistle indicated that air from inside the station was now being sucked out into space, slowly depressurizing and de-oxygenating the sector they currently occupied. Kenneth let the shotgun dangle from its sling and readied himself for a vicious attack.

This sector was much smaller than the previous one, and he estimated it would take less than thirty seconds before the room they were in was fully drained of air. Once the enemy breached the door though, the atmosphere would equalize with two more sectors, drastically increasing the total volume of air. He figured if he could occupy the invading force for ninety seconds, they would all become incapacitated from oxygen deprivation and the assault would cease. His finger wrapped around the trigger. He didn't have to wait long for his plan to go into motion.

The boarding party knocked down the second door and a pair of grenades soared through, chased by a swarm of bullets. They were apparently expecting Kenneth's team to be positioned in a similar configuration as the previous breach. In response to the door coming down, Kenneth's men tossed their grenades up high and through to the other side. The enemy fire slackened as they realized the absence of the defenders where they expected to see them, and a bristle of motion went through the formation as soldiers reacted to the grenades being lobbed into their ranks.

Then a series of loud pops brought men on both sides of the door to their knees, blinding eyes and bursting eardrums.

For a few seconds every fighter in the battle was left reeling from the effects of the grenades, but Kenneth's men had prepared themselves, and with their positions on the other side of the passageway, they were able to recover enough to follow up the attack. The six elite operators darted from the corners of their room and began surgically dispatching concussed enemy combatants.

The scene before Kenneth was a thick gray and black morass of bodies and equipment, but his mind was working in overdrive, and he went to task right away. He picked out an enemy soldier writhing on the ground before him. Up close he could make out the Asiatic features of the man's face behind a transparent ballistic visor, lending evidence to confirm his assumption that the Chinese were behind this attack. Kenneth aimed his submachine gun into the gap between the man's neck guard and his face shield and fired three shots. The hollow tip bullets entered at a downward angle through the man's clavicle, shredding his heart and lungs and taking him out of the fight, permanently.

Another armored figure in front of Kenneth was slowly bringing a weapon to bear, but Kenneth drilled a chain of eight shots into the man's neck and face. The series of close-range shots split through the layers of protection, at least one bullet making its way through the man's upper esophagus and impacting his spinal column, dropping him to the ground. Enemy soldiers near the back of the formation had recovered from the cluster of flashbangs and were fighting back. A bullet slammed into Kenneth's face shield. The thick transparent polycarbonate layering stopped the round, but a web of spidering cracks rendered the visor fully opaque. Kenneth flipped the visor up on top of his helmet and fought on.

One of Kenneth's men was eviscerated by multiple sources of concentrated automatic fire, spinning to the ground on top of an enemy he had just slain with a bullet to the head. Another operator from Kenneth's squad brought a ballistic shield up just in time to address the fusillade but was pressed to the ground by the volume of fire before a ragged hole was torn in the shield, followed by more hot lead. Kenneth got down low and sprayed return fire at the advancing foe until his MPX ran dry. He noticed an enemy stirring on the ground next to him, and with no time to reload, Kenneth drew his pistol and executed the man with a point-blank shot to the back of his exposed neck.

    Looking up, Kenneth saw a pair of enemy soldiers approaching him. Kenneth stole the initiative and leapt directly at the two men. He slammed into the body of the first man, working the barrel of his Glock 21 up underneath the man's face shield then pulling the trigger, painting the transparent ballistic glass red as the .45 caliber round blew apart the man's cranial cavity. The second man nailed Kenneth with a spray of gunfire, knocking him to the ground. Kenneth felt pain scream through his body as some of the bullets bit through soft armor and caught his exposed flesh, but he fought on.

    Sweeping out with his leg, Kenneth caught the other man's legs and toppled him to the floor. The enemy warrior trying his hardest to end Kenneth's life landed on his back, feet towards Kenneth. Kenneth aimed between the man's legs, up into his unarmored crotch and lower buttocks, then sent round after round into the vulnerable area, his bullets punching up into the man's lower abdomen and taking the fight out of him.

    Kenneth was beginning to feel the effects of the dwindling oxygen levels as more and more of the life-sustaining air drained out into space. His heart was racing, and he was struggling to catch his breath, the physical exertion of combat coupled with the thinning air making him slightly dizzy. He would have noticed his ears popping as well if he wasn't still half deaf from the flashbang explosions. The other men locked in battle around him were clearly experiencing similar effects as the fighting had taken on a more sluggish pace. Looking back to the sealed door, he saw a team of three enemies had moved past the scrum and were frantically working the cutting torch on the next door.

They must have realized the situation they were in. At this point even if they sealed the hole, they would soon be going hypoxic, so they needed to breach into the next sector which would still be full of oxygen rich air.

Kenneth began extricating himself from the mass of bodies when an enemy soldier ran at him, weapon raised. Kenneth turned to face the attacker, expecting to be put down by a stream of close-range automatic gunfire, but right before the man pulled the trigger, his boot landed on a pile of loose shell casings, and he lost his footing. The charging man slipped backward, his submachine gun firing wildly into the ceiling. Dozens of mortal struggles across myriad battlefields had taught Kenneth to exploit any bout of luck to the fullest extent possible. He brought his pistol around and emptied the rest of the magazine into the man's side, arm, and shoulder, then scurried towards the men torching the other door.

As he made his way to the torch crew, he passed an enemy soldier kneeling above Master Sergeant Stackowitz, struggling to bring a pistol to bear on Stackowtiz's neck. Kenneth wrestled his Benelli shotgun out from under the MPX submachine gun, the two weapons clattering against each other on separate slings. The compact shotgun boomed as he hip-fired three rapid loads into the enemy soldier, knocking him sideways. From the cloud of lead balls hitting the man, most glanced off armor but a few found their way through exposed areas, fatally wounding him.

Kenneth covered the rest of the ground in under a second, the enemy troops with their backs turned didn't even register his arrival. He placed the muzzle of his shotgun against the back of the first man's helmet and pulled the trigger. The shot, similar to the one that had previously put hole in the space station wall, blew the ballistic-rated helmet apart, scattering skull fragments and brain matter across the door. The second man was one of the pilots, not wearing any body armor. Kenneth planted the last shotgun load center mass, ripping the man's torso open and mangling his lungs and heart. The man fell in a heap against the door.

By now Kenneth's temples were pounding and his vision was losing sharpness. The third man who had been cutting into the door turned to face Kenneth, torch still roaring. The Chinese operator dropped to a low stance, wielding the torch as a weapon. Kenneth went for his combat knife but before he could reach it his opponent made a swift lunge, slashing with the blazing torch. Kenneth had to duck and roll to evade the lethal tool, following his dodge up with a double leg takedown. The other man went down and rolled to the side, still gripping the torch. The man arced the torch up in the air and drove it down towards Kenneth's sternum. Kenneth's hands shot out and held the torch back, but the man had propped himself up on his shoulder and was using part of his bodyweight to press the torch down.

Kenneth considered a headbutt, but his foe's head was well protected by the ballistic helmet and face shield. With no other viable recourse, Kenneth pressed back against the other man's wrists with all his strength. His vision was blurring, and his lungs were screaming, his breaths were drawing in no oxygen. He knew, however, that his opponent was in the same dire straits. Kenneth was determined to outlast the man he was facing. SEALs were tough, and Kenneth was as tough as they came.

Kenneth had been pushed to the brink of death during BUD/S, and among other things, had walked away with a high level of comfort working in a state of oxygen deprivation. Between jumping into the pool with his hands and feet tied, struggling with all range of SCUBA equipment failures, and the relentless harassment of SEAL instructors forcing his head below water, he had spent countless hours exerting himself physically while being unable to take in breaths of air.

Staring into the other man's eyes, Kenneth could tell a lack of oxygenated blood reaching the man's brain was taking its toll. Kenneth felt the man's grip slacken, the torchlight winking out as pressure from the man's palm lifted off the actuation lever. Kenneth seized on the weakness. He twisted the torch out of the man's grip, flipped it around, then pressed it down on the man's neck while reigniting the torch flame. The 4,000 degree Fahrenheit flame easily scorched through flesh, a short gurgling howl of horrendous pain marking the soldier's passing.

As his opponent's body went limp, Kenneth looked back at the tangle of armored soldiers behind him. He saw the lone survivor from the rest of his team pressed with his back against the wall struggling to reload his weapon with one hand while the other hung limp at his side. Two Chinese soldiers were stumbling towards him, but before they reached their quarry, they fell to the ground and did not get up. Shortly after, Kenneth's comrade slumped over, a loaded magazine tumbling from his loose fingers.

Kenneth felt himself on the verge of succumbing to the dark embrace of asphyxiation, when he had what could only be described as a moment of divine inspiration. He grasped the oxygen line on the oxyacetylene torch and ripped it from its socket on the pommel of the torch handle. Pressurized oxygen began spewing out. Kenneth stuck the tube in his mouth and inhaled deeply, his lungs filling with the 99.5% pure oxygen gas. Kenneth took another breath and felt as if an electric jolt was shooting through his body. Clarity returned to his vision and his brain fog lifted, his limbs feeling reenergized. Kenneth shuffled over to his man that he had seen go down moments earlier, dragging the cutting torch's fuel tank apparatus with him. He reached the prone form, recognizing the face of Captain Brown. He shoved the oxygen line through Brown's pursed lips while holding his own breath.

A few seconds later, Brown's eyes flicked open, and he sat bolt upright, looking around in distress. Kenneth knew they couldn't survive there much longer, even with the oxygen source. The pressure had dropped dangerously low and prolonged exposure to the near vacuum would begin to disrupt their vital bodily functions. Kenneth pulled Brown with him towards the sealed emergency door to the next sector, trading inhalations from the oxygen tube. He tried to speak into his headset, but his throat was unable to form any meaningful sounds. Melissa must have understood the situation from her security camera overwatch, because the door slid open before them. Fresh air burst through into the corridor, and Kenneth and Brown practically fell through into the next sector, the door quickly slamming back shut behind them.

    Kenneth sucked in huge lungfuls of the normal air, his body relishing the nitrogen rich gas that it was more accustomed to taking in. A station medic rushed to his side and began peeling his armor off to diagnose his wounds. Kenneth was exhausted both physically and mentally, his mind slipping into a light fugue as he questioned how he was still alive.

CHAPTER 33

Alan Shepard Space Station, Geostationary Orbit
May 7, 2033
1210 Hours CST

The clean sterility of the debrief room belied a sense of calm and control that Maria was certainly not feeling inside. Upon returning to Shepard station, minus over a billion dollars in hardware and one priceless pilot, she thought that she had had a rough time, but when she got the full picture of the carnage that had taken place in the narrow corridors of the station, she felt a sharp sense of vulnerability. The violence was one thing, but the implication of the attacks, which the Department of Defense had officially determined were orchestrated by the Chinese Communist Party, left her with a sense of cold dread.

Maria was joined by the carrier crews and a few other pilots who had not been with her on the mission. General Ironwood had come up to the station to address the spacebound personnel directly and was joined by a General Yarnell, who Maria thought had played a role in the 2030 air battle with China. Ironwood spoke with an air of anger and frustration, but he maintained a spirit of stoic determination.

"Your mission up here, now more than ever, is of paramount importance. War is now unavoidable, and domination of space will decide who emerges victorious, and possibly whose cities will be reduced to radioactive rubble."

He paused as the assembled flight teams bore the weight of his words.

"Down on Earth, there are enough ground-based

electronic and ballistic defense measures now that no one will be able to land a meaningful strike. In order to hit these Commie bastards hard, we need to neutralize their satellites and orbital defenses. If we can bring our space-based ordnance into play unopposed or carve a path for our ICBMs, we think we can bring the CCP to heel without deploying the weapons of mass destruction. If not, well, we're prepared to do whatever it takes. At the same time, this means that it is absolutely critical that we not allow the Chinese to gain the upper hand out here. Doing so could mean the destruction of our nation."

At that the general's iron gaze passed over his small audience.

"We've been given a practically unlimited budget to continue building out the fleet up here. As of now we are on a full war footing and will be conducting combat maneuvers as such. I'm counting on you all. Your country is counting on you all."

CHAPTER 34

Alan Shepard Space Station, Geostationary Orbit
May 25, 2033
1535 Hours CST

Two weeks had passed since war had broken out. It was clear to Rob from the news stories streaming up to him on the station that the United States and China were indeed at war. Despite the fact that blood had already been shed on both sides though, neither belligerent seemed willing to rush headlong into an escalation of violence. Rob suspected that each nation was subtly working to make sure they had all variables in their favor before launching an all-out offensive.

The world appeared to be splitting off into predictable factions, heralding the arrival of the infamous "World War III" that had been a global bogeyman for decades now. The NATO members were contractually bound to ally with the United States, not that they would have chosen any differently regardless of treaty documents. Russia, India, and China formed the foundation of the opposition, while all the countries in between were being bid on like goods at an auction.

Meanwhile the biggest battles were taking place economically or within cyberspace. The world was still plowing forward under previous economic momentum, but pretty soon trade disruptions would catch up to the supply chains and life would take a hard turn for billions of people. Rob had been told though that the most critical fight would be the one in space, as the outcome up here would determine who would hold nuclear dominion over the Earth.

That made his work all the more important, and he labored with a sense of purpose and motivation he had never felt before in his life. The asteroid had eventually been positioned in the planned orbit where the mining teams could conduct their work from the station. The price paid to get it there had been high, but it looked as if the dividends paid out would make it very much worth it. The density of rare metals was beyond what any of the scientists had predicted, and the demand was higher now than ever before.

Construction of an orbital processing facility wasn't slated to begin until next year, but that timeline had been moved up and the work was underway now to begin refining the harvested minerals into a usable state while still in space. This would allow the raw material to be put to use right away, fabricating the military machinery that would be needed to win the war.

In this regard, Rob thought that his side had a big leg up on their enemy. He was confident that through his efforts and those of the miners he was working with, the United States could leverage this edge and ultimately restore the balance of power to bring humanity back to an era of relative peace. No matter what perceived advantages were had though, he knew there was a long road ahead.

PART III

CHAPTER 35

Alan Shepard Space Station, Geostationary Orbit
October 15, 2034
0930 Hours CST

The muted glimmer of gold flakes speckling ragged chunks of raw ore held Rob's attention as his gaze followed his fresh harvest from asteroid 2006 FV35 on its way to the comminution circuit. As the matte gray rocks fraught with pinpricks of yellow passed under the intense white LED lighting, the interspersed micro pockets of pure gold sparkled like stars in the night sky. Rob turned his head left for a glimpse out the porthole window and his eyes were met with actual stars, the brilliant dots of light appearing sharper than they would in any terrestrial night sky, the distant beams unperturbed by atmospheric diffraction.

After more than a year and half in space, most of it spent 22,000 miles from the surface of the Earth in a Geostationary Orbit aboard the United States Space Force Alan Shepard Space Station, Rob had become largely accustomed to the unnatural nuances of life in outer space, yet views like this never ceased to enthrall him. With the proper celestial conditions and alignment, the view of the stars from Shepard Station was downright stunning. Rob had the sensation of being put in his existential place as he dwelled on the natural wonder of photons traveling countless miles over tens of thousands of years to paint the picture before him.

Returning his focus to the job at hand, Rob carefully monitored the load of gold ore on its journey through the series of mills and sifters that would separate out the junk rock tailings, yielding a purer product for the processing plant. Left in a pensive mood from his brief cosmic contemplation, Rob reflected on how he was currently carrying on a pursuit as old as civilization itself. The ecstasy of gold, as it were, had enraptured humans throughout history. From the earliest tribes to the Spanish Conquistadors, from the California Gold Rush to the more environmentally destructive modern industrial mining, gold had always held value to humanity, though its uses had undoubtedly transformed.

The gold that Rob was working to extract from the massive mineral-rich asteroid was directly feeding the development of critical military hardware and assets. While gold was far from the most prevalent element used in the construction of the combat aircraft, spacecraft, missiles, and satellites being produced en masse, it was still a crucial ingredient in forming the highly sophisticated computer electronics packages that turned these lumps of precision engineered metals into lethal instruments of war making. With international tensions at their boiling point, this production was more important now than ever before.

The situation as Rob understood it had reached a stalemate of sorts, although it was far from a cold war given that active military engagements were taking place. The United States and her NATO allies on the one side were facing down the powerful BRIC alliance of Brazil, Russia, India, and China. After a decade of martial escalation not seen since the days of the Union of Soviet Socialist Republics, this time largely centered around space-based offensive and defensive capabilities, the major global powers had once again fallen into what appeared to be a gridlock of nuclear parity.

Extensive arsenals of missiles and other ballistic weaponry capable of mounting conventional, nuclear, or biological warheads were positioned all around the globe and scattered among the thick bands of orbiting satellites. Meanwhile, vast networks of defensive assets taking the forms of anti-ballistic missiles, kinetic kill vehicles, and even high-energy lasers ensured that no nation could launch a nuclear strike with the confidence that they would actually destroy their target.

The concept of mutually assured destruction had evolved to match the universal abandonment of the Outer Space Treaty of 1967. The real power now lay with the satellites and other orbital platforms, which had naturally become prime targets for military action. These militarized satellites had defenses of their own, be it active anti-missile countermeasures or the more subtle security through obscurity, but they were still vulnerable to attack.

Just as one should expect a nuclear launch against a city or country to be met with a response of equal or greater magnitude from the enemy, an attack against an entity's satellites would elicit a similar measure of retaliation. Modern society had become so dependent on satellite technology that an all-out assault on the multinational satellite infrastructure would be just as direly destructive as a nuclear war.

And yet, the pressure of a dwindling supply of natural resources butting up against an ever-increasing global population was driving nations to take risks to secure their future survival. Despite the sound logic of M.A.D., Rob was sure that if one side ended up in a position to cripple or utterly destroy their opponents before a terminal counterstrike could be launched, they wouldn't hesitate to seize the opportunity and eliminate their competition.

These thoughts depressed Rob, even more so knowing that he was now thoroughly embedded in that military-industrial complex. He remained dedicated in his labor though, motivated by the knowledge that if his nation's enemies were able to take the upper hand, it would likely mean the end of him, his community, and their entire way of life.

CHAPTER 36

City of Xinzhou, Shanxi, China
October 15, 2034
2300 Hours China Standard Time

Qing Li felt his hands tremble as worked the mouse and keyboard of his manager's desktop computer, downloading a series of files onto a tiny USB thumb drive. The tenebrous office was illuminated solely from the light of the dual computer monitors, whose contents was reflected on Qing's round glasses. Qing knew that he had finally come across a piece of critical intelligence, information that could at last allow him to strike back at the regime that had stolen so much from his family.

Qing was born in 1994 in the Northwestern Chinese city of Jiuquan, where his parents served as menial laborers for the Jiuquan Satellite Launch Center. His parents had to travel sixty miles by shuttle bus each way to go between their home in the city and the remote launch site. Combined with their long working hours, this meant that they had little time to spend at home caring for their child. When Qing was five years old, his mother became pregnant with his younger sister. Despite his family falling under the draconian one-child policy of the time, his mother refused to give up her child-to-be and went ahead with the birth in secret.

Thus, the beautiful Hai-Ping Li was brought into a world in which her existence was illegal. Since Hai-Ping did not officially exist as a Chinese citizen, Qing's mother was unable to arrange for any form of childcare or apply for a maternal dispensation from work, and so the job of caring for the infant fell largely on the young Qing. Qing developed a deep love for his baby sister and embraced his responsibility with tender devotion.

When Hai-Ping came of age to begin attending school, her parents realized that they could not deprive the girl of an education by continuing to hide her from their overbearing government, so they arranged for her to be taken in by a family of Uyghur Muslims in the neighboring Xinjiang province. The Uyghurs treated Hai-Ping as their own child, providing an environment in which she could grow and thrive. Qing and his parents were even able to see her once or twice a year, an occasion they looked forward to more than anything else.

Meanwhile, Qing, who had developed an impeccable work ethic after taking on many parenting responsibilities at a young age, was excelling in his studies. After scoring top marks on his Zhongkao, the Senior High School Entrance Examination, he was selected by the Chinese Communist Party to become part of an infiltration program aimed at placing Party assets within prominent American defense contracting companies in order to eventually deliver valuable intelligence and classified information into the hands of the CCP.

With the full support of The Party, Qing was enrolled in a Mechanical and Aerospace Engineering program within the Henry Samueli School of Engineering at the University of California, Irvine. There, he took on the more American name of David Li, and blended in as just another student from abroad seeking an education at a prestigious American university. His ultimate goal was to continue on to complete a Master's or Ph.D. program and then find employment at a company like Raytheon or Northrop Grumman within the United States.

The Chinese government kept assets like Qing in line and focused on their state-mandated objective with persuasive collateral. In this case, Qing's parents were kept under a watchful eye by The Party, and it was understood that if Qing did not perform his duties to the best of his ability, his parents would suffer for it.

Years of indoctrination coupled with implicit threats moved Qing to pursue his mission with diligent loyalty, but after spending time in California, interacting with the Americans and other foreign students from around the world, he began to see The Party for the heavy-handed autocracy that it was. Despite these observations, he resigned himself to the path ahead, fearing for the wellbeing of his parents and knowing that a comfortable position within The Party hierarchy awaited him upon his eventual success. This all changed after his junior year.

In the summer of 2015, Qing went home to visit his family in China during a break between his junior and senior years of college. When he spoke to his family in person for the first time in a year, he learned that the Uyghur family caring for Hai-Ping had been forcibly sent to a re-education camp along with thousands of other Uyghurs. In these camps, the Uyghurs were held as prisoners and subjected to relentless political propaganda meant to erode their cultural identity, while living in squalid conditions. Many were pressed to perform hard physical labor, while some were raped, sterilized, or otherwise tortured.

Word had reached Qing's parents that upon arriving at the camp, Chinese guards noted the distinct ethnic disparity between Hai-Ping and the Uyghurs she was living among. The eighteen-year-old Hai-Ping was declared a race-traitor and subsequently beaten to death.

This news had broken Qing's parents, and it nearly broke Qing as well. He spent days in deep mourning, the intense grief leaving him unable to eat or sleep. As his thoughts circled around existential injustice, one emotion slowly overtook his sadness: rage. Rage at the camp guards, rage at the government that had sent them there, rage at the communist party that sought to impose its rigid dogma on all others under penalty of death, rage at what the state of China had come to represent.

When Qing returned to California, his mission had transformed. He would continue with his current pursuits at the behest of the CCP; however, his endgame was no longer to simply serve The Party. He vowed he would work himself into a position of trust where the right opportunity, once it came along, would allow him to repay The Party for the cruelty it had inflicted upon him.

Near the end of his senior year as an undergraduate at UCI, Qing took the first step on his road to revenge. He knew the CCP kept assets like him under surveillance, so he would have to act carefully to not cast suspicion upon himself. When a campus wide career fair was held, Qing attended, making the rounds to all the major tech and aerospace companies, as would be expected of him. Qing knew from discussions with his peers that the American Central Intelligence Agency recruited heavily from the top universities to fill its ranks of shrewd analysts with bright young college graduates. The CIA did not have a traditional booth like most companies present, rather a representative from the agency held a stack of brochures with information for an off campus recruiting event taking place that evening.

Clearly Qing could not be seen speaking directly to a member of the CIA, so he devised a plan to make contact inconspicuously. Qing wrote down on a piece of paper a link to a dark web messaging drop box that could only be accessed through a Tor browser by individuals with the exact address string of twenty randomized alphanumeric characters. Below the link he scribbled a brief note:

I am a CCP agent. I want to flip.

As Qing was making his way out of the large hall housing the career fair, he turned his head down to stare at his phone, appearing to not be watching where he was walking. He then brushed up against the CIA recruiter, knocking the man's pamphlets to the floor. Qing apologized profusely and began gathering up pamphlets for the man, slipping his own note on top of the stack while doing so. He then handed the stack back to the CIA representative, holding eye contact with the man a couple seconds longer than would have been socially comfortable. His heart was racing as he strolled out of the great hall, nervous that his message wouldn't be received, or worse, that a CCP informant would discover his treachery.

He waited two discomposing weeks, anxiously checking the dark web server each day, before a response arrived. It appeared that the CIA was willing to talk. Over the next months, Qing slowly developed a working relationship with a CIA handler, who took great pains to thoroughly understand Qing's history, his psyche, and his motives for turning traitor. Qing remained in the United States that summer, attaining a prestigious engineering internship slot at the American aerospace company SpaceX. Eventually accepting his story, the CIA handler began to develop Qing into a double agent.

Bolstered by a renewed mission focus, Qing acquitted himself assiduously in a Master's degree program in Aeronautics and Astronautics at the Stanford University School of Engineering. Upon graduating, he already had a job lined up as a systems engineer at the Lockheed Martin Space Division. Five years later, he was recalled to China, delivering to his government an array of plans, designs, and engineering methodologies that were highly classified, yet ultimately inconsequential in the broader scheme of things.

Back in his estranged homeland, his talents were put to use at the China Academy of Space Technology, where he worked on maintaining critical satellite orbits. His parents were kept under general protective custody by the state "for their own safety" to ensure his continued loyalty to The Party. From his position within CAST, he covertly slipped tidbits of potentially useful intel back to his CIA handler in Langley, Virginia. Up until now though, none of his revelations had been of any consequence.

Three months prior, Qing had been brought in on a project to equip a Huanjing weather satellite with orbital nuclear strike capabilities as part of an ongoing development of The Party's space-based arsenal. While Qing was only serving in an ancillary role on the project, he was still privy to many of the specifics. Furthermore, he knew the exact personnel who would have access to the full operational design domain documentation, including detailed diagrams of the satellite's upfit modifications and the onboard weapons targeting and launch computer. This, he assumed, would be quite valuable to the Americans in their fight against the totalitarian despots administrating his country.

In his years of sleeper service to the CIA, Qing had been practicing his espionage fieldcraft, and it was a trivial matter to piece together his manager's computer password from surreptitiously observing a few of his morning login sessions. From there, it had only been a matter of opportunity. With a major deadline looming, his team had been permitted to work beyond the facility's normal security curfew, well into the night. Qing had stuck around the office, fighting his nocturnal fatigue while posing as the ever-dedicated worker. Just before midnight, his manager finally called it quits, and Qing made his move. That brought him to this moment, alone with unfettered access to his manager's desktop and the military secrets contained within.

After several fretful minutes, a popup window indicated a successful file transfer. Qing plucked out the memory stick, slid it into his briefcase, and began making his way casually to the exit. Sweat trickled from under his arms and down the back of his neck, and he prayed that he would not encounter the scrutinizing gaze of one of the stony-faced security personnel. He made it out of the facility without incident, and as he transported the nondescript USB drive to the dead drop where it would be picked up by some unknown deep cover CIA operative, he couldn't help but feel that he had just signed his own death warrant.

CHAPTER 37

Ruth Gorge, Alaska
November 22, 2034
0300 AKST

Glittering ice shards showered Cody Jackson, the patter of pieces bouncing off his helmet punctuated by the percussive hammering of his Petzl Nomic ice pick pounding into the unyielding wall of ice before him, glinting in the Alaskan moonlight. Cody was twenty feet above his last protective gear placement, an eleven-centimeter screw bored into a thick column of ice, and was getting desperate for an opportunity to make another placement. The unforgivingly steep and featureless section of ice he was ascending was difficult enough to cling to as it was, and he couldn't hang for the prolonged seconds it would take him to drive in another screw.

Cody was currently leading a pitch of arduous alpine climbing, meaning that it was his responsibility to create anchor points to run one of his twin ropes through as he moved upward. He had various pieces of equipment dangling from his harness that he could place into the rock and ice that would hold him if he fell. At least he hoped they would hold him. If he were to fall, he would plummet twice the distance to the last piece of gear he had placed before the rope tethered to his harness and attaching him to his belay partner down below arrested his motion.

Halfway up the three-thousand-foot cliff face marked by patches of ice and hard-packed snow, Cody considered his position. The metal spikes of the crampons attached to his booted feet dug mere millimeters into the ice, offering just enough support for him to hold the rest of his weight with the ice tool in his left hand, lodged half an inch into another patch of rigid ice. If he were to slip now, the results could easily be disastrous. He lacked the confidence that the previous screw he had buried into the ice would hold the force of a forty-foot whipper, and even if it did, the razor-sharp equipment he wore on his feet and held in his hands provided an additional avenue for injury.

Cody reflected upon the first rule of lead climbing on ice: Don't fall. Channeling this simple slogan, he flung his right arm up, casting the ice tool grasped in his right hand as far as he could reach. The curving, jagged stainless-steel blade mounted on the carbon-fiber tool cleared a thick bulge of ice above Cody's head and bit into a layer of soft ice atop the bulge. Visceral vindication vibrated throughout his body, the tool sticking solidly. Cody raised his left foot and scraped his crampon against a verglas sheet while hauling himself up with his right arm, tightly gripping the firmly planted ice tool. He quickly matched with his left arm, giving him two points of contact to drag his body over the small ledge.

Now seated on the bulging ice, Cody worked a long aluminum screw into a robust icy pillar, then backed up his anchor by wedging a spring-loaded camming device into an adjacent crack in the stony cliffside. He clipped an end of the nylon personal anchor system running from his harness into each of these newly placed pieces of protection, then called to his belayer one hundred feet below through the radio headset integrated into his above-the-ear high cut ballistic helmet.

"I'm in direct. You can take me off."

This indicated to his belayer, Captain Mason, that Cody was now secure of his own accord and no longer required the safety of Mason's belay. Next, Mason would prepare to follow Cody's path, gathering the gear he had placed into the mountain while Cody reciprocated with a belay from his new perch.

The two men were part of a six-man squad making their way up the imposing Moose's Tooth rock peak in Alaska's

Ruth Gorge, the concluding exercise of a month-long training program they had been undertaking based out of Talkeetna. The program was designed to prepare the CIA Special Operations Group task force for an extreme infiltration operation in the Himalayan mountains. Cody and his teammates had not received a full briefing of what the exact mission would entail, only that they would require the use of finely honed mountaineering and alpine climbing skills.

Cody, a native of Billings, Montana, had been pulled from his DEVGRU SEAL team to join this SOG unit due to his comprehensive climbing background. Cody had grown up playing in the mountains, and years of Montana winters had hardened him to the most severe elements. Other members of the squad were joining him from the Army Rangers, Delta Force, and even the 10th Mountain Division. Every man on Cody's new team had extensive experience navigating and fighting in alpine environments, and the past month had transformed them so that they were now not only warriors, but elite mountaineering athletes.

Five weeks ago, Cody had met his SOG unit in Talkeetna, where they wasted no time diving into their exhaustive bouts of training. The men were already in peak physical condition, so the program focused on sharpening the skills that would be required to ascend the bleak Himalayan terrain, as well as acclimatizing to high altitudes. They spent long days rucking full loads through deep snow fields and up steep glaciers, climbing up rock and ice alike while wearing full combat kit. After the first couple weeks, they shifted their schedule so that they operated exclusively during the night, reflective of the future mission parameters.

As part of the training, the team made two successful summits of the monumentally daunting Mt. Denali. At 20,310 feet, Denali stands as the highest mountain in North America. The combination of its high altitude and far northern latitude creates some of the coldest, most brutal weather conditions on the planet, and the back-to-back early winter ascents marked an achievement that would impress even the most masterful mountaineers.

The SOG team was outfitted with top-of-the-line gear from companies like Black Diamond, Petzl, and Outdoor Research, and world renown alpinists were brought in to help them train and impart hard-earned wisdom. Nutritionists monitored the men to ensure that their body fat levels didn't drop too low, a base layer of subcutaneous fat being a vital asset in winter wilderness survival.

Cody gazed out across the fields of snow glistening under a full moon, the landscape accentuated by rows of rugged granite obelisks. Looking to his left along the rock wall of the Moose's Tooth, he glimpsed the other two-man rope teams making a similar climb. Whatever the mission may entail, he felt ready.

Mason radioed in, "I'm ready to climb."

"Belay's on," Cody replied.

"Climbing."

"Climb on."

Cody began to pull the pair of ropes through his belay device in time with Mason's ascent, pausing every now and then while Mason unscrewed ice screws from their icy holds, plucked aluminum nuts and cams from cracks and crevices in the stippled granite, and re-racked slings and carabiners on his harness. The soft howl of the wind through the snowy rock features was Cody's only companion.

Soon, Mason was pulling himself over the bulge to join Cody on the precarious ledge. Cody transferred the few remaining pieces of protective gear he still had on his harness over to Mason's, then without further fanfare, Mason took over the lead and continued the duo's upward progress.

CHAPTER 38

Talkeetna, Alaska
November 24, 2034
0900 AKST

After the first full night of rest since Cody and his specially selected squadmates had arrived in Alaska, the elite operators were gathered into a small briefing room with a man and a woman whom they had never seen before. The unremarkable black sweaters worn by the pair gave no clue to the organization they belonged to, but their darkly confident bearing screamed CIA.

"Good morning, gentlemen," the woman began. "My name is Rebecca White, and this is Deputy Director Alex Langmeyer. I'll be your ground branch liaison for your upcoming mission."

Confirmed spooks.

Rebecca brought up a presentation on the room's digital wall screen.

"HUMINT sources have suggested the existence of a Chinese quantum computing and cryptography development lab constructed last year within the Shigatse Prefecture in the Tibet Autonomous Region. We have validated a high probability location via satellite imagery located near the Nepalese border in the Himalayan range. The facility appears to be very well protected, built atop a small mountain plateau. It's totally off the grid, no signals going in or coming out. A single road runs north along the only stable approach, while the rest of the compound is surrounded by a sheer two-thousand-foot cliff face. The Chinese must assume that the cliff band negates any ground approach outside of the single heavily guarded road. Your job is to prove them wrong."

Rebecca cycled through new slides on the presentation.

"An aerial insertion is out of the question, as that airspace is fully locked down by Chinese assets. Your team will fly into Kathmandu, posing as Canadian mountaineers looking to make a winter ascent of Everest. You will follow the Tama Koshi river north by motor vehicle to the end of the highway, then proceed fifty miles on foot across the Chinese border to your target."

The CIA woman moved on to the facility infiltration rundown.

"A stealthy entry to the facility is imperative. We don't know exactly what level of security force they have stationed on-site, but we don't want you shooting it out with a platoon of Chinese special forces. Based on the satellite imagery, we have a decent idea of where their air-gapped storage servers are located. Ironically, we think these servers will have little in the way of security encryption. The Chinese are relying on the physical security of the location to protect their data and won't want to slow down their on-site operations with superfluous measures. Our friends at the NSA have put together a set of manual devices to grab data from these servers. If you can get into the server room, the NSA programs will do the rest. We don't know the exact nature of the physical interface, so the team has put together seven different sets of devices containing the same program. Once inserted, it should only be a matter of minutes to get what we need, then you extract the way you came in. You will remain transmission silent until you return to Kathmandu. I will give you a contact on the ground there to regroup with. You will have no other support during this mission. If anything goes wrong, the United States will not acknowledge any affiliation."

Rebecca turned off the digital presentation.

"Now, gentlemen, I believe you have a plane to catch."

Another Thanksgiving with the family missed, Cody thought to himself. One more addition to the lengthy list of sacrifices the defenders of freedom must make.

CHAPTER 39

Kathmandu, Nepal
November 25, 2034
1202 NPT

Upon touching down in the vast sprawl of Kathmandu, Cody and his team wasted no time gathering up gear and procuring transportation out of the city. Fortunately, the amount of supplies needed for an ascent of Mt. Everest matched the volume of the bulky crates they had flown in with, and no eyebrows were raised. A closer inspection would have revealed pounds of military hardware interspersed throughout a collection of technical climbing equipment and winter survival gear.

Inside the packed, bustling airport, the SOG team ran into another group of westerners there on a climbing trip. Even a world war wasn't enough to stifle the towering ego of a career mountaineer. With all the big peaks already conquered, repeating traditional routes during the harsh winter months had become the new path to glory in the high-altitude mountaineering world. Cody and his comrades briefly swapped stories with the group of excited climbers before moving on. The actual alpinists were awed by the true tale of the SOG unit's off-season ascents of Denali and the Moose's Tooth, leaving the unquestioned impression that undercover CIA operators were real-deal mountaineers.

The team exited the airport and rented an old beat-up 2010 model Volkswagen van, then began meandering through the dusty, densely packed streets of Kathmandu. The air was comfortably warm, a welcome change from the Alaskan chill.

The pleasant temperature, though, was offset by the oppressive odors and fetid atmosphere of pollution. The van, filled to the brim with men and material, soon wound its way out of the vast metropolis and the warriors settled in for an eight-hour drive ahead.

Snaking through the crests and valleys of the Nepalese countryside, the CIA soldiers were treated to stunning vistas of lushly forested hills backdropped by titanic mountain monoliths. As they slowly went up in elevation, the nearby trees gained glazes of ivory frost to complement the distant snow-capped peaks.

Darkness had fallen by the time they arrived at the end of the line. The men disembarked and geared up, leaving the van parked on the side of the road. They had all slept on the plane and were ready for a full night of rucking through rugged Himalayan foothills. There were no trails to speak of, so the squad followed a rough valley carved out by a modest tributary to the Tama Koshi river.

The SOG unit crossed the Chinese border around four o'clock in the morning, the steep terrain and delicate bushwacking making for slow going. The group made camp in a narrow gulley along a snowy hillside, taking time to carefully camouflage the site. Cody's wrist-mounted altimeter read 10,400 feet. They rested, slept, and refueled their bodies during the daylight hours, resuming their trek once the blanketing cover of night returned.

The second night brought light snow showers and a stiff breeze. With temperatures hovering around twenty degrees Fahrenheit, exposed flesh quickly felt the bite of the frigid alpine air. The intense physical exertion of moving through the rough terrain with an eighty-pound load kept all the men sufficiently warmed though. They made another twelve miles, carefully skirting the scattering of small valley villages. Six inches of snow now layered the ground, and the rear man in the line was tasked with obscuring their tracks. It wouldn't fool an astute tracker on the ground, but it would hide their trail from prying satellites. Each man was also draped in mylar foil to mask their infrared signature from thermal imaging.

By the third night, sparse stands of trees gave way to low scrub bushes and stretches of moribund stony plains. Alternating bouts of snow and freezing rain constituted Mother Nature's attempts to strip away the hardened operators' resolve, but none were willing to yield. At an altitude of 15,000 feet, the stoic squad found a cramped cave to shelter inside of and wait out the following day.

After arduous trekking up and down steep snowy ridges, the fourth night brought Cody and his crew to the base of the cliff that marked their objective. The team dug out a small burrow in the deep snow and prepared to commence their assault upon the impregnable mountain face the following night.

CHAPTER 40

Langley, Virginia
November 28, 2034
1030 Hours EST

Rebecca was seated in a seventh-floor conference room at the Central Intelligence Agency headquarters in Langley. Gathered with her were five other high ranking intelligence officers, including the director.

"Do you really think they can pull this off?" a man in a crisply pressed black suit who Rebecca knew only as "Kingston" asked.

"Yes, I have full confidence in my team," Rebecca responded curtly. "It's a difficult mission, but if anyone in the world can get it done, it's these boys."

"We've been trying to track their progress via satellite, but a storm system seems to be moving in and there's too much cloud cover to pierce through," a technical officer added to the conversation.

"But we know they made it to the target location?" inquired the director.

"Well, no," Rebecca answered. "We won't really know anything for at least a few more days. I'd expect them in Kathmandu no sooner than the third."

"And for the sake of our friends here, Ms. White, could you remind me what we think we can accomplish with the data at this…facility?" the director asked.

"Intel suggests that the Chinese have been making leaps forward in quantum computing development. Specifics of what goes on in this research center are locked down tight though. We can't get a picture of where exactly they stand. I shouldn't have to explain why it would be catastrophic if the Chinese achieved fully functional quantum computing before us. All of our encryption protocols could be rendered useless overnight. We need to know where they're at, and if they are ahead of us, we need to use what we can get from them to catch up."

The director merely grunted with acknowledgement at this statement.

"Furthermore, we know the work being done there is integrated closely with their cryptography branch. The two fields being interrelated, of course. Now, more salient to present operations, we suspect that within the databanks of this facility, we could find the encryption algorithms used to secure their orbital nuclear launch computers. You're aware of the Huanjing satellite intel we picked up from our source in Xinzhou last month, correct?"

"Yes, I am."

"We believe we can commandeer that satellite with a local hack, but we need something for the NSA cyber guys to work with to construct the hacking profile."

"Okay, I see where this is all going," a gray-haired woman whom Rebecca didn't recognize ventured. "If we can take control of one of their satellites, we could be well positioned for a nuclear strike against China. So, what's our next move?"

"For now," Rebecca replied, "all we can do is pray that our ground branch team is successful."

CHAPTER 41

Shigatse, Tibet Autonomous Zone, China
November 29, 2034
2015 Hours China Standard Time

Cody and his squadmates geared up in silence. Cody donned his arctic camouflage coveralls over his down-feather winter suit. He had on a light armor vest underneath containing level IIIA aramid plates. The lighter plates wouldn't stop a rifle round, but it was better than nothing, and he couldn't afford to be climbing with heavy steel or bulky ceramic armor plates. He secured spikey crampons to the rigid soles of his thickly insulated leather boots. His harness was cluttered with nuts, cams, screws, alpine draws, and other climbing accessories.

Cody's backpack contained a sixty meter long 7.8mm climbing rope, a half-liter of water, a couple of energy gel packets, a compact trauma kit, and a small assortment of other combat sundries. He also stuffed in a large down parka that he and his climbing partner would share for use while belaying. His pair of short, serrated ice axes were strapped to the outside of the pack. A lightweight white and gray patterned Heckler & Koch MP7A1 submachine gun with a thick suppressor lay flush along his lower right side, tightly held in place by a two-point sling. He only carried two spare magazines filled with the weapon's 4.6x30mm armor piercing ammunition. A suppressed SIG Sauer M17 service pistol chambered for 9mm NATO rounds completed his arsenal.

Cody fixed the strap of his white ballistic helmet and pulled down his L3Harris Ground Panoramic Night Vision

Goggles, the quad tube setup giving him a wide field of view in either lowlight or infrared modes. Activating his throat mic, he checked in with his teammates over the PELTOR headset radio network.

"Sierra Four, ready op."

Mason would be his climbing partner again for this ascent. The two men had trained together rigorously in Alaska, and Cody was confident they could scale just about anything the mountain could throw at them. Mason would be carrying the NSA data theft package, one such package being held by each of the three climbing pairs for redundancy. The teams left the rest of their food and gear stashed at the base of the cliff and began trudging upwards through powdery waist-deep snow to begin their ascent. Cody took a reading from his wrist computer. Altitude: 16,348 feet. Temperature: 9 degrees Fahrenheit.

The men had a general idea of what their line up the daunting escarpment might be based on studies of the satellite imagery, but it was impossible to truly tell the quality and viability of a route without feeling it out in person. The first few hundred feet proved to be relatively easy scrambling, and the SOG operators didn't even bother roping up. They soon came upon a nearly vertical rock face, and the real climbing began in earnest.

The three teams spread out to attack the headwall before them, each finding a workable line amidst the cryptic slab of feldspar schist and leucogranite. Tying into the twin climbing ropes, Cody took the first lead. He delicately clawed and wedged his ice tools against the coarse rock to gain purchase and move himself upwards, pausing to place protective gear and clip one of his ropes in when the formation allowed. Climbing in the moonless blackness, relying on the night vision tubes affixed to his helmet, Cody strained to make out features through the green-hued panorama. It complicated things, but they had been climbing exclusively at night for the final weeks in Alaska, and he had grown accustomed to the ordeal. One hundred and fifty feet later, Cody anchored himself atop a stolid stone shelf, then

Mason followed him up.

Mason took the next pitch, a craggy rock passage interspersed with columns of grayish ice. Cody dutifully fed the rope through his belay device, wiggling his fingers in between moves in a vain effort to stave off the creeping cold. While in motion, keeping warm wasn't an issue. It was during the stationary belay that Cody felt the icy touch of the frigid air. He had pulled thicker covers over his thin climbing gloves and wrapped himself in the belay parka, but it was barely enough to suppress a shiver.

The pair continued moving upwards, swapping leads, as they went. The terrain varied from trivial to impassable, and in a few instances Cody and Mason had to traverse over to follow a line found by one of the other teams when no path availed itself. After three hours they were nearly halfway up the wall. The wailing wind whipped mercilessly as Cody moved higher up, and during strong gusts he had to pause and press himself against the cliff, praying that the turbulent gales would not pluck him off the wall. Dull numbness in his fingers and toes had become a constant companion.

Resting on one of the more generously sized ledges, Cody and Mason extricated energy gel packets to provide their bodies with some meager offset to the caloric price of the relentless ascent in the draining cold. In his body's fuel-deprived state, the chalky chocolatey glucose solution blended with electrolyte and amino acids tasted better than the finest gourmet meal. Ending the brief respite, Cody launched up a steep icy couloir. His movement meticulous and methodical, Cody maintained a regular cadence up the section of pure ice as he dug in with crampons and ice tools. Hand, hand, foot, foot. Keep the heels down, derive power from the legs. Maintain three points of contact at all times.

The climbers had entered into a band of streaky clouds, and small snowflakes swirled about in the sporadic squalls. Visibility dwindled and Cody could see no more than ten feet ahead of him through the grainy green viewing window, but that was all he needed. The thousand-foot drop below him was now obscured, not that it mattered to Cody. He had banished any sense of vertiginous trepidation long ago.

The band of ice seemed to stretch on forever, and as Cody reached the end of his rope, no stable belay location had revealed itself. In that case, Cody would have to create one himself. He drove his remaining two ice screws into the thick sheet and anchored off of them before radioing for Mason that he was up. Cody dangled against the ice while he belayed his partner up, nothing but thin air beneath his feet.

Mason reached Cody and gave him a knowing grin as he pulled up to the tenuous belay station, the four tubes covering Mason's eyes giving him an eerie alien appearance. Cody transferred from a top belay to a lead belay and Mason continued the pair's progress up the ice.

Ten minutes later, still hanging from his two ice screws, Cody heard a frantic call from Mason.

"Rock, rock! Falling!"

Cody flattened himself against the wall just in time for a stony flake the size of a shoebox to thunder past him, spraying chips of ice as it bounced down the steep face. A split-second later Cody was jerked upwards as the ropes caught Mason's fall and the force transferred down to Cody. Cody rose a foot into the air before plopping back down, his clove-hitched anchoring ropes tugging violently against the ice screws. Miraculously, the gear held. Cody immediately called out to Mason.

"You good?"

"Yeah, I'm good. Just ripped a loose flake off. My last cam held though, bomber piece."

Cody hadn't seen any errant gear chasing the rock down, so Mason must not have lost anything. His ice axes would be attached to his harness by elastic leashes, keeping the vital tools secure. The men wasted no further time dwelling on the fall. Mason was already moving back up, reclaiming lost ground.

The rock grew looser as they neared the top of the cliff, decent sized chunks coming dislodged from time to time, but none as large as the flake that had caused Mason's fall when it came off. Fortunately, thin channels of ice provided a stable enough route. Cody battled through perilous pitches with sketchy steps, working his way up some featureless portions of the cliff through sheer force of will. After three more hours of some of the hardest alpine climbing he had ever done in his life, the angle of the slope began to slacken, and the crest came into view through brief gaps in the swirling mist.

"Sierra One is at the top, securing breach point," Cody heard his team leader call out over the squad radio channel.

Cody estimated he and Mason were still fifteen minutes from topping out themselves.

"Sierra Three, be there in fifteen Mikes," Mason reported.

"Sierra Five, likewise," the third climbing pair echoed.

The bellowing wind had picked up even more by the time Cody scrambled onto flat ground, bringing it to a raging tempest. Snow flew sideways past him. At least these conditions would further conceal their infiltration. Cody belayed Mason up the final stretch then the pair joined their other squadmates by a hole Sierra Two had cut in a privacy screened chain link fence. Cody stashed his rope and climbing gear in his backpack, while freeing his MP7 from its sling and sliding the two spare magazines into the backpack's shoulder straps where they would be more accessible.

"Stack up for entry," Sierra One subvocalized through his throat mic. "Go."

The team of white-clad operators slid through the opening in the fence and crept through the blizzard, eyes and submachine gun muzzles tracking every angle. They didn't actually know where the server they sought would be located, but they had a prioritized list of structures to check based on intel analysis. The ghostly figures split into two teams to form up on opposite doors of their first target building. Cody tested the handle on the door he was leaning up next to. Unlocked. He supposed with all the external security measures, there was no need to keep the doors locked on-site.

"Now."

On that call, Cody pulled open his door with his left hand while keeping his weapon raised with his right. His three-man split wrapped around the corners, inspecting the room. Meanwhile, the other half of the SOG team worked through the opposing end of the building. The indoor space offered a welcome respite from the nasty winter weather, although dressed for the subzero temperatures as he was, Cody found the heated quarters almost stiflingly warm.

"Clear."

"Clear."

"No joy."

"Regroup and let's hit Bravo."

The two trios reunited back out in the savage storm and began slinking along the fence line to their next objective. The team was in between structures when Sierra One called a halt. Two bundled up individuals carrying what looked like QCW-05 submachine guns were strolling between buildings up ahead. The forward members of the team already had their weapons up, sights trained on the pair of hunched over guards pushing their way through the stiff squall.

"Let 'em pass."

Sierra One's voice came out little more than a gargled whisper through Cody's headset. If one of these guards were to turn their head and spot Cody's team, they would instantly be riddled with high velocity 4.6mm bullets. If they held their course, they would remain among the living, and the SOG team's element of stealth would remain intact.

Soon, the guard patrol was out of sight, and the ground branch operators continued with their mission. They stacked up outside a set of double doors and made another quick, uneventful entry. The inside of this structure was relatively cold compared to the previous one, barely above freezing according to Cody's thermometer. That was a good sign. The hard-working server machines would more than likely be kept in a well-cooled environment.

Cody heard the voice of Sierra Five sound out, "Bingo."

The men finished clearing out the structure, then regrouped at Sierra Five's find.

"This has gotta be it," Sierra One agreed. "Let's get to work, boys."

Sierra One dug out his hacking kit and began trying to match a device to the multi-pronged ports of the server. The rest of the squad took up covering positions while he worked.

"Got it," Sierra One announced, inserting the matching drive.

The men waited with tense impatience while the program on the memory drive executed and downloaded as many files as it could hold. A sudden blaring klaxon made Cody jump.

"Fuck," one of the operators exclaimed.

"Goddammit, I thought they said the program would be undetectable!" Sierra Two complained.

"They say a lot of things," Sierra Six replied, leaving the implication hanging in the air.

"Okay this one's done. Three, give me your set, we need to run one more download for backup," Sierra One ordered.

"You sure boss? Seems like we should get the hell out of here," Mason protested.

"We're not leaving without a backup download," Sierra One stated with finality.

Mason passed his set of devices to the team leader, who inserted another drive in to run the same routine. The NSA code seemed to be able to work through any lockdown response the alarm may have triggered.

"Alright it's done," Sierra One advised the team. "Let's get the fuck out of here."

Fingers hovering over triggers, the SOG team exited the structure and began making towards the fence line. Cody had flipped to his IR viewing frame to cut through the dense snowfall. The group made it to the next structure over when thermal signatures began registering fifty yards ahead, blocking their path to the fence.

"Take 'em."

The words had barely left Sierra One's lips before the SOG operators opened up, quiet streams of 4.6x30mm gunfire ripping into the thermal blobs ahead. After the first few bodies dropped, a wild rattle of 5.8x21mm rounds began flying back in the Americans' general direction. Unable to make out the faint phantoms against the dense haze of snow, none of the enemy soldiers were able to land a shot on target. The SOG men continued firing while advancing toward the fence, cutting down the rest of the Chinese response force.

Cody and his group of unseen death-dealers continued on at a hurried pace. They had nearly reached the breach in the fence when a truck veered by and skidded to a halt, more Chinese fighters bailing out and opening fire. The SOG members caught in the open hit the deck and began returning fire, while Cody and a couple others dove for cover behind a nearby structure. The new arrivals must have been utilizing thermal imaging of their own, as their fire appeared much more focused.

"We need to wipe these guys before we can rap' off," Sierra One stated. There was no way they could set their ropes and descend the cliff with enemy shooters still present.

Cody heard a guttural grunt and glanced right to see Mason's prone form splayed out, his gun lying dormant against the snow. *Win the fight first, then render aid.* Cody snuck around the side of the building, swapping in a fresh forty round magazine while he moved. He dashed around the side of the now stationary truck and came up on the other side facing a line of Chinese soldiers sending rounds downrange towards his teammates. Cody took a moment to line up his shot. With two brief taps of his trigger, he dispatched the first two enemy soldiers, short bursts of the 4.6mm copper-cased steel projectiles drilling through the brain stems of each man and dropping them to the ground.

A third soldier spun around to face him, weapon raised, but Cody placed a tight grouping of sustained fire high-center mass, tearing through clothing and armor and rending open the man's chest cavity. The other men in Cody's squad picked up on the tempo change and pressed forward, putting down the remaining enemies with disciplined bursts of submachine gun fire.

Cody sprinted back to check on Mason. He rolled his partner over, revealing a series of ragged, bloody entry wounds. One of them went straight through Mason's eye socket. The man was dead, no doubt about it.

"Let's go, let's go!" Sierra One called. "Set up your rappels."

"Sierra Three is KIA," Cody informed the team.

Sierra One acknowledged the news with a solemn "Copy."

Cody dragged Mason's limp corpse through the fence then dug his partner's rope out of the deceased warrior's backpack, knotting it together with his own to form his rappel line. Stowing his weapon, Cody hooked the meeting point of the joined ropes around a suitable rock then threw the tow coiled ends over the edge, the sixty-meter lines unraveling as they spilled down the cliff.

Next, Cody threaded each end of the rope through his rappel device and secured both his and Mason's harness to the device with carabiners and a nylon sling. Cody hefted Mason's dead weight onto the front of his own body and began walking back over the lip of the cliff, making his descent. Leaving Mason's body behind for discovery was not an option.

Cody worked his way down the mountainside in sixty-meter stints like this, pausing at the end of each rappel to pull the rope down and set it up all over again for the next stretch. The icy wind berated him all the way, while Mason's face pressed against his own, his single staring eye devoid of life. The other two pairs of operators were running simultaneous rappels, each man descending on one strand of the rappel line while his partner counterbalanced him.

In some spots, Cody reached the bottom of his rappel line without a suitable ledge to support him while he set up the next rappel. In these instances, he would have to build an anchor into the rock and ice using pieces of climbing gear while hanging freely from the rappel ropes, then transition himself and Mason to the new anchor before pulling down the rappel line. The normal climbing ethic dictated that one should avoid ever leaving gear behind on the mountain. Given Cody's in extremis situation, he had no qualms ignoring this precept and leaving ice screws or camming devices buried in the icy massif as needed to facilitate his rappels.

Two exhausting hours later, Cody finally reached the deep snow slopes marking the base of the escarpment. The other four members of his team were there to meet him, and they helped haul Mason's body back down to their gear stash. The men hastily dug a shallow grave into the frozen, rocky earth and laid Mason to rest. Cody made sure to retrieve Mason's memory device laden with the valuable intel the man had died collecting. Hopefully his body would remain undiscovered in perpetuity.

Gathering up the rest of their stashed gear, the ragged operators beat their way through the sticky snow and the stinging storm, determined to reach the cave they had stayed at on the third night of the mission. Five hellishly grueling hours later, the weary operators collapsed inside the safe haven of their cave. The sun must have come out hours ago, but with the thick storm clouds still overhead, they could barely tell. Despite the violent resistance the storm presented to the team's movement over the hilly terrain, it gave them cover to avoid the prying eyes of searching drones and helicopters. Once their position in the cave was set up, Cody fell into a deep sleep.

CHAPTER 42

Shigatse, Tibet Autonomous Zone, China
November 30, 2034
1200 Hours China Standard Time

Cody awoke an hour later to muffled cries of pain as Sierra Five extracted bullet fragments from Sierra Two's shoulder. The men passed the rest of the day buried in their small cavern, ravenously devouring pre-packaged meals. In the late afternoon, they could hear the storm breaking, soon followed by the intermittent beating of helicopter rotor blades overhead.

When darkness fell, the team resumed their stealthy slog back towards the Tama Koshi river. If thermal imaging drones weren't scanning the countryside before, they surely were now, and the men moved with gentle care, staying under their mylar foil shielding. When they made it back to the tree line the next night, the stout conifers provided welcome concealment.

After one more night bivouacking under a thick grove of pines, the SOG squad finally emerged into the valley of the Tama Koshi. Making their way along the steep hillside, the soldiers found the van they had left along the fading roadway days before propped up on crude hunks of limestone, missing all four tires. The men glanced at one another, wordless acknowledgement passing between them. Without speaking, the five tireless operators began walking down the road.

Four miles south, the team came upon a small village. There were no automobiles in sight, but villagers were tending to packs of mules. The SOG team leader approached one mule herder and pulled out wads of Rupee notes, trying to purchase mules for his team. The village herder laughed at the paper, which held little value to him. Sierra One produced his MP7A1 submachine gun and held it out for the other man to inspect. Suddenly the villager was eager to do business, and for the price of the weapon and two partially filled magazines, the SOG team left the village riding atop steadfast mules. Eventually the appearance of military-grade hardware in the remote village would arouse suspicion, but Sierra One was banking on being out of the country by the time that bit of gossip filtered down to the foreign intelligence circles.

The group rode on, keeping the mules at a steady clip. They rode through the night, taking turns sleeping in the "saddles" they had crafted out of winter clothing and climbing slings. The following day, the team reached a larger village, this one containing a number of motor vehicles. Sierra One bartered some more, and after giving up the mules and one more MP7, the SOG unit was tearing down the dusty highway in a rusted-out van with a full tank of gas.

Nine hours later, the van full of filthy, unkempt operators arrived at an inconspicuous CIA safehouse thirty minutes from Tribhuvan International Airport in Kathmandu. They had taken a lengthy detour to ensure they weren't being followed, and the van was running on fumes by the time they pulled up to their destination.

More of an apartment, the safehouse sat sandwiched tightly between rows of other dilapidated dwellings. Inside, they were greeted by a short, wiry Nepalese man who spoke fluent but heavily accented English. The hovel was warm and dank inside, little in the way of interior decor aside from rickety wooden furniture. Sierra One asked for a way to contact Rebecca White, and the local CIA asset ushered the group over to a laptop in the corner surrounded by a few other pieces of electronic equipment.

With assistance from the diminutive Nepalese man, Sierra One established what was supposedly a secure satellite call with a CIA communications specialist back in Virginia. After a minute, the call was routed to Rebecca.

The ground branch liaison answered with a terse, "White speaking."

"Ms. White, this is the Sierra team. We have the gold and we're at the safehouse in Kathmandu. We lost Sierra Three, but everyone else is doing okay. How soon can you get us out of here?"

"I can have a Gulfstream wheels down in four hours. Will that work?"

"Yes, ma'am."

"Okay, until then stay put at the safehouse, we need you to keep a low profile until it's time to bug out."

"Copy that."

"I'll contact you when the jet is thirty minutes out."

With that, Rebecca ended the call.

The team spent the next hour checking over their gear and monitoring the feed from the discreet surveillance system set up around the house. After another hour scrutinizing the feed, Cody's instinct began nagging at him. He called over his team leader and explained his observations.

"See these guys? Here-" he said, gesticulating to a spot on the laptop screen, "and here. They've been hanging out more or less in the same spot for thirty minutes now, with perfect sight lines to the front door of our house."

Sierra One frowned while he examined the pixels making up the external camera feed.

"Dammit," the team leader cursed under his breath. "God damn it. Somehow the MSS got eyes on us. We're compromised."

"These guys must be keeping an eye on us while they wait for backup," Cody guessed.

"Yeah, I think so. Alright, we gotta move. Can you get White on the line?"

"Yes, sir."

The Chinese Ministry of State Security, the Communist Party's intelligence branch, would certainly have eyes and ears in a bustling international hub like Kathmandu. Cody couldn't think of how exactly the MSS had made his team, but it was irrelevant now.

Rebecca answered the second call with an annoyed "Yes?"

"Ma'am, we've been compromised. Chinese Ministry goons are watching the safehouse. We're going mobile."

"No, wait! You need to stay put. If you get yourselves lost in the city, we'll never be able to locate you."

"Okay, do we have any other assets in the area that can help us out here? We don't currently have the firepower to go toe-to-toe with a squad of MSS hitters."

"Mmmm," a hum of consternation escaped Rebecca's lips. "I don't think so. Let me check on a few things, and I'll get back to you in fifteen. For now, just stay put. There should be a small armory in the safehouse if you need to augment your capabilities."

"Copy."

The call cut, and Sierra One turned to the Nepalese housekeeper.

"Where's the armory?"

"This way, sir," the man replied, "It's not much, but it may help."

The Nepalese man led the Sierra team members to a drab basement and opened a large safe, revealing a row of four M4 Carbine rifles and a stack of loaded magazines. The SOG men distributed weapons and ammo, each operator ensuring that the rifle they held had a full magazine inserted and a round chambered and ready to fire. Three minutes later a voice call notification came in on the laptop.

"It's White. I talked to my counterpart over at MI6. They have a detachment of E Squadron operators in the area. They're on their way to the safehouse now with transportation. By the time they arrive, they can take you directly to the airport and your plane should be almost there."

Sierra One addressed the CIA woman. "Copy that, ma'am. We're getting antsy here though. I really don't want us to be sitting around with our thumbs up our asses waiting to get smoked out by Chinese SOF."

"Trust me, Sierra One, you need to stay put. The Brits will get you to the airport, you just need to hold out for them."

Cody, listening in, could read between the lines of Rebecca's orders. If his team went off on foot through the city and got taken out, the invaluable hard drives would be impossible to locate. If his team got wiped at the safehouse, though, there was a chance that the MSS teams wouldn't know what they were looking for, and the CIA could get a team of their own in to retrieve the hard drives later. Cody understood well that the mission came first, and if they had to stay put, they would stay put.

"Understood, ma'am."

"Good luck, Sierra One."

"Thanks," Sierra One started to reply, but Rebecca had already hung up. The Sierra team leader turned to address his men. "Alright boys let's get ready for some company. Four, you keep an eye on the surveillance. Five and Six, cover the door from the kitchen with the rifles. Two, you're with me, we'll position at the foot of the basement stairs."

The small apartment had only one door in or out. The windows were too small to squeeze through, so it all came down to a single choke point. The Nepalese CIA man had a pistol drawn but was hanging back away from the door. Cody had one of the MP7 submachine guns across his lap, loaded with a single magazine containing the remaining twenty-five rounds scavenged from all the partial mags. The team had donned their light armor vests and ballistic helmets over their casual western attire.

Five minutes later, Cody saw two black SUVs pull up on the street outside. As men wearing brown and gray patterned fatigues holding short-barreled rifles poured out, the civilian foot traffic took this as a sign to clear out of the area.

"They're here," Cody announced to his team. "I count twelve tangos, rifles and body armor."

Cody kept the team apprised of the situation in real time

as he watched one group of six men lining up outside the door that was just around the corner from the room he was seated in. The other group of six men were hanging back, guns held at high-ready.

Before the Chinese kill team had set up their breach, Cody heard the roaring of an engine coming from the streets outside. Moments later his video feed displayed a large pickup truck barreling down the dusty road. Men from the rear assault element began turning their heads just before the pickup bowled into them. The truck plowed through all six men, knocking some to the side and pasting others against the hard packed dirt. Limbs snapped and bodies rag-dolled, the truck only beginning to slow after impacting.

The weaponized vehicle hadn't even come to a stop when all four doors flew open and grubby-faced men dressed in local garb leapt out. The new arrivals were toting decked out Heckler & Koch G36 carbine rifles and they immediately began executing the splayed out MSS vehicular ramming victims with sharp bursts of gunfire.

"The Brits are here!" Cody yelled.

The rest of his team had already sensed the shift in the battlefield dynamic and were rushing out the door. They shoved the door open from the inside, turning the tables on the breaching team arrayed outside. The MSS breachers were pivoting to address the new threat from the MI6 operators when the SOG commandos burst through the doorway. The four American operators hosed down the MSS team with fully automatic sprays of 5.56mm bullets. Less than twelve seconds had passed since the arrival of the British E Squadron, and twelve MSS assaulters lay dead in the dirt.

The driver of the E Squadron's pickup truck shouted to the Sierra team members while gesturing towards the bed of the truck, his voice heavily laden with a South Yorkshire accent.

"Hop in the back. I 'ear you boys got a plane to catch."

Cody scampered outside to join his comrades, and the five soldiers hoisted themselves into the empty truck bed, carrying only their weapons and the two sets of hard drives they had worked so hard to obtain. As the truck squealed away from the scene of acute violence, Cody spotted the Nepalese CIA agent darting down an alley. The man would have to trigger the sanitation process now that the safehouse was compromised.

Dry wind rustled at Cody's loose-fitting clothes as he and his team members maintained an omnidirectional vigil from their position tucked low against the bed of the pickup. Their British driver navigated the choked streets of Kathmandu as swiftly as he could, weaving through a conglomeration of people, motor scooters, rickshaws, and other cars. Cody caught sight of a black van that rounded a corner and began following their path with a similar level of alacrity and pointed it out to his team lead.

Sierra One bent down near the open rear window of the truck's cabin and yelled to be heard over the ambient clamor.

"Is that one of yours?"

Sierra One pointed at the tailing van.

"No, mate," said one of the E Squadron operators. "We came alone."

Sierra One consulted with Sierra Two. The van was about fifty yards behind them, with copious civilian traffic in between. Sierra One called back through the rear window.

"Can you take a sharp turn up ahead then come to a stop?"

"You got it, mate," the driver replied.

One variegated city block later, the truck whipped around a corner then slowed to a stop. Other road users continued flowing past like the current of a river around a rock. Soon, the black van careened around the corner and was met by the raised firearms of Sierra team. The SOG warriors opened up without hesitation, thoroughly perforating the large vehicle with a torrent of lead. Shards of glass and sprays of blood marked the demise of the driver and front passenger. A wounded man wobbled out of a side door and Cody laid him out with a double tap from his MP7.

"Now punch it! Let's go!" Sierra One shouted to their own

driver.

The pickup lurched forward amidst the loud revving of the engine and took off, back on course towards the airport.

Ten minutes later, the truck was approaching a gate leading to the tarmac. A dark blue SUV was parked sideways, blocking the gate, with armored figures covering behind it. Avoiding the roadblock, the MI6 wheelman veered left down a dirt road, then walloped through a small ditch onto a dusty field with dry yellowing grass. The truck rumbled along the open field, traveling parallel to a chain link fence that surrounded the runway strips, the driver seeking some weakness in the barrier.

Finding what he was looking for, the E Squadron driver hooked the truck out wide away from the fence, then turned directly towards a section where the soil had eroded away underneath the fence, digging out the foundation and leaving the fencing canted at a forty-five-degree angle. The driver stomped the accelerator, dirt spitting up from behind the rugged tires, and the truck rocketed towards the fence.

The growling truck plowed into the fence with a kinetic jolt, flattening the bowed-out section and crossing more open ground onto the paved runway. Cody and his teammates in the back of the truck tightly braced themselves for the impact but were still bounced up inches off the truck bed as it clobbered the crooked fence. After reaching the pavement, the truck raced towards the far end of a runway where a sleek Gulfstream G800 jet had just landed and was slowing to a taxi.

Cody noticed the blue SUV that had been blocking the gate was now on the runway as well, accelerating towards them on a perpendicular intercept path.

"Two o'clock! Light that fucker up!" Cody yelled to his team, who needed no further prompting.

The Sierra operators rested rifles along the roof and railing of the truck and began taking deliberately aimed semi-automatic shots at the SUV. The quiet coughing of Cody's MP7A1 was drowned out by the boisterous booms of a quartet of M4 Carbines. Hissing cracks signaled supersonic rifle rounds being fired in return from inside the large SUV. The windshield glass spider webbed from a hit, but the up-armored MI6 pickup truck with its run-flat tires resisted the onslaught. E Squadron shooters began engaging from the passenger side windows, and as the two clashing cars neared, the hostile SUV was soon overwhelmed.

The SUV coasted to a swerving halt, the driver having taken at least one incapacitating hit. The British-American contingent continued pouring on fire as they blitzed past the stationary vehicle. Cody's submachine gun ran dry, and he drew his sidearm, adding 9mm NATO rounds to the fusillade.

The Gulfstream jet had just rolled to a stop when the pickup truck filled to the brim with tier one special forces operators pulled up alongside it. The Americans in the back hopped out and filed up the entry ramp. Before boarding, Sierra One turned to the E Squadron leader.

"Thanks, you guys really pulled our asses out of the frying pan there."

"Cheers, mate. Bloody good show."

With that the special MI6 unit sped off, no doubt looking to disappear back into the labyrinthine streets of Kathmandu.

The pilots of the CIA-owned Gulfstream jet wasted no time getting into the air, the engines never having even been shut off following their landing. After the initial steeply banked vertical ascension, Sierra One stepped into the open doorway to the cockpit to converse with the pilots.

"Where we headed?" the Sierra team leader queried.

"Berlin," the co-pilot answered back.

"So that's what, seven hours?"

"Six and-" the co-pilot was abruptly cut off by a shrill beeping tone coming from one of the cockpit instruments.

"Aw shit, we're getting lit up with a radar lock!" exclaimed the pilot.

"SAM launch detected," the co-pilot announced.

"Strap in back there, we're going evasive!" the pilot called to the SOG passengers.

Sierra One staggered back to his seat just in time for the jet to break into a stomach-churning climb, coupled with a tight turn that shoved the operators sideways.

"Dumping chaff," the co-pilot tensely stated.

Seconds later, the beeping stopped, and the plane's trajectory evened out. Cody heard the co-pilot making a call over his radio.

"CENTCOM One, this is Zulu Xray Niner. Our airspace is hot, requesting immediate assistance."

Cody couldn't hear the other side of the conversation, but after a few seconds of silence, the co-pilot closed with a simple "Copy."

The jet continued its steady climb through a layer of clouds. Two minutes later, the treble warning tone from the cockpit started up once more.

"Fuck, we're getting locked up again," the pilot cursed.

"I'm picking up two bogey's closing fast!" the co-pilot cried out, an edge of panic in his voice.

"Brace yourselves!" the pilot ordered, preparing for another harsh maneuver.

Just before the pilot threw the jet into a sharp twist, the beeping alarm ceased for the second time.

"They're...they're gone," the co-pilot announced in disbelief. "Two new contacts, IFFs reading friendly.

From their perch at 60,000 feet, a pair of F-25 Storm Crow stealth tactical fighters descended through the stratosphere, having once more demonstrated their technological dominance of the skies. A flicker of motion caught Cody's attention, and he glanced out his porthole window to see one of the elegant, streamlined fighter jets matching velocity and settling in beside the Gulfstream.

Breathing out a long sigh of relief, Cody closed his eyes with no intention of opening them back up again until he was on the ground in Germany.

CHAPTER 43

Alan Shepard Space Station, Geostationary Orbit
December 10, 2034
1000 Hours CST

The station briefing room was more packed now than it had ever been before. General Yarnell paced slowly along the presentation floor, preparing to review the plan of action for the mission ahead. General Ironwood was even in attendance, standing rigidly off to the side. Scanning around the dim space, Maria noted that most of the station security operators were in attendance, in addition to every single combat pilot and flight crew member not on an active patrol at that moment.

Yarnell took a deep breath and dove in.

"Ladies and gentlemen, we have been green lit for a major operation that we will execute in six hours' time. For this op we will be coordinating with elements on the ground with the goal of achieving a successful nuclear strike against a string of cities within eastern China."

Yarnell stood for a moment while the assembled personnel digested his words. Maria saw a few looks of surprise, but most remained impassive, as if they had been expecting this since the outbreak of the conflict. Yarnell resumed.

"Intelligence assets have ID'd a Chinese satellite registered as an environmental monitor that is holding eight rocket propelled nuclear warheads with full launch capabilities. It is currently in a highly elliptical low Earth orbit, passing about 400 miles over mainland China at its perigee. We will send a screening force of twelve Supernova fighters and eight Perseid carriers to intercept at twenty-five degrees ahead of perigee and deploy an EVA team to dock with the satellite. The docking team will perform a local hack to take control of the firing computer. Once the satellite is in position over China, we will launch all eight warheads at targets below. While this is going on, aerial and amphibious forces in the Pacific will be assaulting the Chinese-held Sakishima Islands to capture or destroy five recently installed kinetic hit-to-kill anti-missile sites. If we can take control of at least three out of the five sites, not only do we take those defenses away from the Chinese, but we can turn them against the mainland to negate Chinese defensive anti-ballistic missile launches. We will have a window of around one hour where a successful nuclear hit is virtually guaranteed. All teams are to begin prepping immediately. Let's end this war. Dismissed."

CHAPTER 44

40,000 feet above the East China Sea, Pacific Ocean
December 10, 2034
1403 Hours JST

Captain Harlow marveled at the endless deep blue hues of the Pacific Ocean through the cockpit canopy of his venerable old Boeing F/A-18E Super Hornet single seat multirole fighter jet. Harlow and his squad were tasked with eliminating a group of hardened defenses located within the Yaeyama and Miyako island chains. The mission objective was to claim superiority over the airspace and clear the way for an amphibious assault on the Chinese missile defense installations that had been built on five of the islands in the archipelago.

These clusters of small tropical volcanic islands had been annexed from Japan by the Chinese Communist Party after they invaded Taiwan in 2028 to forcibly bring the island nation under full Chinese governance. By taking control of this string of islands just off the eastern coast of Taiwan, China denied Japan, and her close ally the United States, an important strategic position from which to contest their new claim. Once China had displaced most of the local Japanese populace, the remote isles served as suitable sites to construct robust defensive strongholds, including a crucial addition to the Chinese missile defense program.

Harlow understood the strategic value of wresting these military redoubts from the Chinese; however, it was not clear to him what the United States Indo-Pacific Command hoped to accomplish with this isolated aggression. Without support of a broader Pacific campaign, it seemed to him that the islands would be quickly retaken. Then again, he knew it was unlikely his mission briefing had painted the full picture of the operation.

Harlow and his combat wing had launched from a carrier strike group in the Philippine Sea and had been joined by a contingent of USAF Storm Crows scrambled from an airbase in Okinawa. The Storm Crows, along with their XQ-58 Valkyrie drone complements, would provide assistance cutting through any Chinese aerial threats that came to meet them. The Navy Super Hornets, each loaded for bear with four AGM-84K SLAM-ER precision guided cruise missiles, would decimate the ground targets. The F/A-18s were also running a pair of AIM-9X Sidewinder short range air-to-air missiles along with fully loaded M61A2 20mm Vulcan cannons, but Harlow did not anticipate engaging any enemy aircraft directly. His squad was also joined by a contingent of similarly outfitted F-35C Lightning IIs that had been catapulted off the deck of a mighty carrier as well.

"Specter One for Overlord Actual," Harlow called over his headset.

"Go for Overlord Actual," a deep voice responded.

"Specter elements are five Mikes out from max range to target group Alpha. Confirm we will continue to close to one five zero miles for 99% hit probability."

"Confirmed Specter One."

"Thank you, Overlord. Specter One out."

Harlow had barely finished the exchange before a new set of voices cut in over the communication network.

"Wolf Two to all units. We have bogies burning in hard from the west!"

"Copy, Wolf Two. Sword, Wolf, Hawkeye, move up to engage. Specter, Zeus, Diamond, hold course and maintain targeting protocols."

Harlow followed the impending aerial engagement on his computer's team-linked radar detection portrayal of the battlespace. Clusters of friendly icons slowly increased in speed to meet an approaching array of hostiles while his squadron and the other strike craft continued on their fixed path towards the ground targets. The minutes crawled by as the opposing forces screamed towards each other at hundreds of miles an hour.

As the radar icons closed in on each other, Harlow imagined the two sides must be grabbing locks and preparing to trade salvos of BVR missile shots right about now. Fully removed from the fight, his headset remained eerily quiet, the radio calls only being broadcast to those who needed to hear them to maintain clear comms traffic for the rest of the force. A terse all-channel call out of "Engaging" from the Wolf squadron leader gave the only audible indication that a dogfight was breaking out in the skies ahead of him.

While the Storm Crows were tangling with the Chinese fighters, his own combat group was entering their designated attack range.

"Specter elements, claim targets and fire when ready. Let's hit those SAMs first," Harlow told his squadron.

"Roger, lead."

"Slammer out!"

Harlow keyed in his own targeting solution and then let loose an AGM-84K, which joined the cluster of other stand-off range missiles on their journey of over one hundred miles towards defensive emplacements on the tropical islands far below. Rocketing through the sky at 600 miles per hour, it would still be a while before the missiles connected with their distant targets. Harlow and his fellow pilots adjusted their approach towards the next set of targets. It didn't take long to reach the next firing point.

"Target group Bravo is within optimal range, fire when ready."

The squadron of Super Hornets each sent one more missile flying off the rail, carrying their 800-pound bunker-busting payloads on a one-way trip towards the militarized tracts of land dotting the vast ocean. The deep voice of the mission commander cut in over the radio.

"Overlord Actual to all strike units, move to engage enemy fighters immediately. We need reinforcements up there."

That didn't sound good. It was hard to tell from his computer picture, but apparently the Storm Crow fighter groups were struggling.

"Specter One to Overlord Actual, be advised we have not yet met our firing parameters for target group Charlie."

"Acknowledged Specter One, launch remaining munitions at current range then double time it over to support Wolf and Hawkeye."

"Hard copy, Overlord," Harlow replied, then switched to his squad channel. "You heard the man, dump those slammers and light up those blowers. Time to join the furball."

Harlow's formation of F/A-18s rolled sideways, firing off their remaining AGM-84K missiles then turning towards their allied aircraft. Harlow's own jet rumbled as he fired his afterburners and blasted through the sound barrier, reaching Mach 1.5 on his approach to the dogfight. As he neared the engagement, he saw that the two sides had entered into BFM combat. Given that his squadron was not outfitted with any long-range air-to-air weaponry, that suited him just fine.

As his fighters roared in to assist, one of the Wolf squadron pilots radioed in.

"Thank God you decided to show up. My fun meter is pegged!"

Harlow and his pilots quickly joined in on the action.

"Hawkeye Five, you have a bandit on your six," Harlow called out to an allied pilot.

"No shit, now why don't you help a brother out and put one of those heaters to use!" The pilot responded sharply, the stress of fighting a losing engagement evident in his voice.

Harlow had let off the throttle as he approached the dogfight, but he fed more power to his General Electric F414-GE-400 turbofan jet engines to pull up behind the enemy that was angling for a kill shot on Hawkeye Five. The distracted

Shenyang J-11 pilot had no time to react as Harlow pulled in for a boresight shot.

"Fox Two."

Seconds later the J-11 erupted into a roiling fireball. Harlow pulled up on his flight stick to avoid the hot debris cloud.

"Bravo Zulu, Specter One. I owe you," a relieved Hawkeye Five exclaimed.

"We're not out of the shit yet," Harlow replied.

As if to emphasize his statement, the urgent beeping of a radar lock detection sounded in his cockpit, and Harlow immediately pulled hard into an evasive maneuver. Visually acquiring the source of the lock, Harlow confirmed an active homing missile was streaking towards him, so he dumped chaff and sped up once again, the familiar G-forces pressing him into his flight seat. The seeker missile detonated harmlessly in the stream of chaff, quieting the missile alert tone in Harlow's ear. Moments later, an old Shenyang J-8 bearing the red star of the People's Liberation Army passed right in front of Harlow.

"Can somebody tag that bastard?" an unknown pilot asked.

Harlow throttled down and went into a tight turn, dragging his cannon reticle towards the slower Chinese aircraft.

"Judy, Judy, this one's mine," Harlow responded.

Harlow felt a visceral satisfaction as his targeting computer matched the aimpoint of the 20mm Vulcan cannon to the J-8's trajectory, like clicking a seatbelt buckle into place or snapping two LEGO bricks together.

"Guns guns guns."

The multi-million dollar flying machine responded to the pressure of Harlow's index finger against the trigger on his flight stick by signaling the fire control module on the M61A2 Vulcan. This actuated a hydraulic drive motor, cycling the six rotary barrels of the cannon as the firing pin hammered out eighty 20x102mm cannon shells in under a second. The SAPHEI shells caught the J-8 across the fuselage and left nacelle, ripping the craft into flaming metal before the pilot could eject.

"Good kill, Specter One."

"I think that's the last of 'em."

"Sword and Zeus, hold perimeter while the other squads RTB for refuel and rearm," Overlord came in over the radio. "Satellite operators are reporting good hits on the ground targets. Nice work team. Now we need to hold this airspace. Diamond and Specter will be on station for close air support. Be advised we're also bringing in some Predator drones for overwatch. Overlord out."

Excitement bubbled within Harlow at the success of his strike and the adrenal thrill of air-to-air combat. Maybe they were finally going to land a meaningful blow against the Chinese menace after all.

CHAPTER 45

Low Earth Orbit
December 10, 2034
1435 Hours JST

Maria had spent the last three hours easing her Supernova into low earth orbit, so the sharp ring from her onboard computer indicating a new hostile contact was almost a welcome break in the monotony. This close to Earth, her sensors didn't retain the incredible performance range that they had in deep space, but the far-reaching satellite and ground-based radar coverage that the United States Space Force held at its disposal more than made up for this. The Extensive network could be easily linked into her squadron's systems to share and utilize the data.

"Satlink is IDing Chinese spacecraft entering an intercept orbit between us and the Baseball," one of the technical crew members on a Perseid carrier in Maria's modest fleet announced. "Baseball" was the designated call for the Huanjing weather satellite they were targeting on this operation.

"Remember, we don't have to take these guys out. Our sole mission objective is to get an EVA team on the Ball. When we're 500 miles out, accelerate at three Gs and we'll blow right past these bastards," Maria iterated to her pilots.

A round of affirmative calls confirmed that all the pilots understood her order. While she had trained with combat groups of this size before in space, she had never run an actual operation with this many ships under her command. Once the Gamma drones deployed from their carriers, her force would number fifty-nine individual spacecraft, plus three short range boarding capsules each carrying a pair of Space Force Extra Vehicular Activity operators.

"Deploy Gammas then accelerate on my mark," Maria stated flatly.

The Gammas would need to be flying independently to even out the carriers' thrust-to-mass ratio for a three G burn. The cluster of blue icons on Maria's IFF computer doubled in size as thirty-nine drone craft detached from their motherships and spread out into an assault formation.

"Mark."

The familiar G-force pinned Maria back against her seat as her Merlin 3F liquid fueled rocket engine came to life, generating thousands of pounds of thrust to speed up her sleek fighter craft. Maria clenched her jaw, maintaining tension through her limbs. Prolonged exposure to these forces would eventually take their toll, but to a veteran combat pilot like Maria, a few minutes of this was nothing.

She knew she had to be mindful of her acceleration vectors in this closer orbit of the Earth. Out in deep space she could blast around in any direction without consequence, but at the edge of Low Earth Orbit, thrusting in the wrong direction could send her burning up into the atmosphere. In a way, the flight patterns in this arena would bear somewhat more similarities to flying the terrestrial skies. The shrill radar lock detection tone sounded in her ear, interrupting her thoughts.

"Multiple missile launches detected," one of her pilots called out.

"Deploy counter-missiles but hold offensive fire. We'll hit them hard right before the merge. The smaller the engagement window we give them, the better. Once we pass them, we'll need to start decelerating to hold our orbit around the Baseball," Maria said, conveying her plan to her team.

Most of Maria's view out of her thick cockpit canopy was dominated by roiling white clouds over the azure oceans of the planet below her, but flashes of light began marking where offensive missile met defensive missile in the exchange of high-tech ordnance. Out of hundreds of hostile missiles, some were beginning to break through and find their targets.

"Gamma group Bravo taking losses."

"Venus Eight is down!"

"Hold fire…"

Maria could see the enemy units adjusting their trajectories to better pursue her squadrons now that it was apparent her force had no plans sticking around for a fight. The enemy's initial intercept course was at a slight angle off of head-on, so they were decelerating hard and would be taking a tight turn to change course. Once Maria's ships passed by, she would have a window of safety before the Chinese pilots came within a reasonable range again. Maria hoped that would give them enough time to carry out the mission unimpeded by hostile spacecraft.

As the enemy ships rapidly approached, Maria confirmed that she had solid weapons locks and scanned through the IFF profiles to try to prioritize targets. There were almost eighty unique tags. Either the Chinese had committed their entire space fleet to address this incursion, or they were substantially outproducing the United States in ship manufacturing. On a relatively even technological playing field, numbers mattered more than ever in a space engagement. Fortunately, Maria's mission did not call for achieving complete battlespace supremacy, but dealing with a numerically superior foe would undeniably make achieving her mission objective more difficult.

Judging that the positioning and timing were appropriate, Maria unleashed the fury of her squadrons.

"Alright cut engines then hit them hard, I want every Jay-tam with a solid lock off the rails!"

Maria and her Supernova wingmates stabilized their flight then began rocketing off missile after missile. The Perseid command operators passed on the instructions to their drone squads, turning them into an impressive force multiplier. Hundreds of missiles passed back and forth over the fifty-mile span between the two sides. Maria's wing thrusters kept the nose of her fighter facing the general direction of the enemy while she passed. The Americans' barrage took a devastating toll on the Chinese fleet, but she lost nearly a third of her own ships in the exchange. She considered adding volleys from her nose mounted cannon into the mix, but with the enemy targets on a steeply accelerating path, the odds of a hit at that range were practically zero.

Relative to the Earth below, Maria's ships were now moving at a blazing 20,000 miles per hour. Most of that velocity however was just serving to keep them in orbit, counteracting the constant "free fall" they experienced as gravity pulled them towards the massive planet. The Chinese ships were in a similar orbital path, so Maria passed them at only 5,000 miles per hour. Still, within minutes her units were already curving over the horizon, putting enough distance between them and the Chinese pursuers to break off from the engagement.

Maria deferred to her computer to plot a trajectory of steady deceleration that would bring them into a matched proximity orbit with the nuke-bearing weather satellite and sent it out to her allies' computers to follow. While her remaining ships were decelerating, the Chinese ships chasing them were accelerating. Currently the American ships still held more velocity, so the distance between the two groups continued to increase, but as that rate of increase slowed it was only a matter of time until the equation flipped, and the Chinese began gaining on the Americans.

If the navigation computer's projections were accurate, it looked like they would have just enough time to deliver a team to the objective before they came under fire again from the hostile ships.

CHAPTER 46

2 Miles off the Northeastern Coast of Ishigaki Island
December 10, 2034
1440 Hours JST

Nick Delgado's heart was pounding in his chest as the BAE Systems ACV-P amphibious assault vehicle carrying him and his squad of fellow Marines jostled through the low waves of the Pacific Ocean en route to their target. They had launched from the large well deck of an America-class amphibious assault ship fifteen minutes ago and were part of a full company of Marines closing in on the Chinese-controlled Ishigaki Island. A simple seating bench ran down the middle of the interior of the armored transport. Nick sat back-to-back with one Marine and had another Marine squeezed in on either side of him, nine total Marines filling the compartment. The tight space was illuminated to match the ambient daylight outside so that their eyes wouldn't need to spend time adjusting once they disembarked.

"You nervous, bro?" a young Marine next to him by the name of Vasquez asked.

Nick had been working at a Little Caesars pizza joint in Detroit, growing bored of life with few promising prospects for the future, when a United States Marine Corps recruiter at the mall enticed him into enlistment. Nick didn't grow up with aspirations to join the armed forces, but at nineteen and fresh out of school, it seemed like just the excitement he had been seeking in life. Besides, his older cousin, Maria, had joined the Air Force about ten years before and she seemed to be loving that. Or was it the Space Force she was in now? He hadn't kept in touch with her, but he figured she must be seeing some action with the war against China going on now.

Boot camp had been a tough ordeal for the lanky youth, but he emerged from the thirteen weeks of hell more fit than he had ever been in his life, beaming with pride at the man he had been molded into. After completing his basic training in January of 2033, the proceeding weeks had quickly turned to drudgery as he went through the motions of life on base. The pace picked up considerably when hostilities broke out with China though, and he had been placed into a Marine Expeditionary Unit stationed in the Pacific theater. Endless drills and exercises had never culminated in an actual combat deployment, until now.

Nick glanced at his squadmate and good friend beside him.

"Yeah man. I mean, aren't you?" Nick replied.

"Nahh, the flyboys gave those fuckers such an asspounding I bet we'll roll up onto the beach and there won't be any baddies left for us to kill," Vasquez proclaimed confidently, an element of false-bravado clearly evident in his voice.

"Sure hope so," Nick mumbled, then went back to checking over his gear.

He turned his rifle over in his hands, a SIG XM5 chambered for .277 Fury ammunition, inspecting each component and ensuring that the weapon was ready for battle. Holding the barrel of the rifle steady with the rail-mounted foregrip, he cycled through the display of his Fire Control System. Some instructor back in basic had joked that with this new generation of optics, there was no need to teach Marines to shoot anymore. The hardware would do all the work for them. In Nick's experience that was far from true, although it was certainly easier to hit a target at 500 yards with the scope's ballistic computer automatically adjusting the aimpoint based on range and atmospheric conditions than with the iron sights of an M16.

Nick continued his checks, running his gloved fingers along the pockets and pouches of his pants and plate carrier rig. The thought came over him that he didn't feel all that safe despite the ceramic armor plates covering his chest, back, and sides; another rounded plate on his off-dominant shoulder that would face his direction of fire; and the ballistic helmet that caressed the upper half of his skull. While the armor pieces were designed to protect his most precious organs from high powered rifle fire, he couldn't help but visualize the multitude of locations all over his body without such protection where a high velocity bullet impact would still end his life.

Nick pushed the macabre thought aside by running through the mission plan again. His platoon would make landfall, then move up the beach in their ACVs until they reached the forested hills. From there, they would dismount and continue on foot, clearing out any remaining resistance while making their way to an entrance to the main missile defense bunker. They would then breach the bunker and clear out the facility, joined by other platoons from the assaulting Marine company entering through different access points. Once the facility was secured, a team of technicians would be brought in to take control of the site. Easy day.

He could hear bits of low conversation taking place inside the small troop compartment, but for the most part the young Marines were stoically silent, focused on the mission ahead. Thus far they had not come under enemy fire, and Nick was beginning to think that maybe Vasquez was correct. The bobbing sway of the transport evened out as the eight super-sized wheels found purchase on the sand of the beach. Nick began to hear the reports of heavy weapons fire outside the armored walls of the transport, and his pulse rose as his hopes for an easy op fell.

The loud echoing pings of bullets and shrapnel smacking into the transport elicited choice curses from the Marines penned up inside. Nick heard the belting thump of the ACV's M2 Browning .50 caliber machine gun returning fire at whatever adversary had them under attack, a crew member aiming the gun via a periscoping camera and a remote control.

"Twenty seconds to the tree line!" one of the drivers shouted for the Marine passengers to hear.

Moments later a loud metallic crack rang out through the hull and the armored transport drew to a halt.

"What the fuck was that?" a Marine blurted out.

"Aw, fuck's sake," sighed another.

"We took something big, the front drive shaft's all fucked up and I can't see shit out the viewport. We're immobilized," stated the crew commander.

"Alright Marines," Nick's squad and platoon leader, Lieutenant Michaelson, boomed. "Time to bail out. Looks like we gotta hoof it from here!"

"Front ramp is jammed," reported another crew member, "you'll have to leave out the back."

The back ramp lowered, ushering in a wave of humid, salty ocean air. Accompanied by shouts of "Let's go! Let's go!" from Michaelson, the Marines filed out the back, rifles raised, and took up positions along the armored vehicle just as they had done countless times in training. The sky was an overcast gray, although whether that was from meteorological patterns or from the heavy amounts of smoke drifting up from the island, Nick could not say. His boots hit the pale tan sand and sank in about an inch, the soft beach welcoming him to what under other circumstances would have been a tropical paradise.

Once the entire squad had disembarked, the Marines began advancing towards the low hills before them. The incoming fire was sporadic, and Nick couldn't tell where any of it was coming from. He was running forward in a low crouch, following his squadmates, when a particularly loud explosion caught him off guard, causing him to stumble. He fell face first, catching a mouthful of gritty sand and banging his rifle painfully on his knee. One of his squadmates turned to check on him but he quickly jumped back up and kept moving. The blunder would normally have earned him some wise cracks from the boys, but no one said a word as they continued hauling ass towards the cover of the hills.

Seconds later, the squad was sheltering against a pile of vesicular volcanic rock. The forest ahead was partially burned out and Nick could see large swathes where few trees were left standing, craters dotting the open ground. Looking along the rocky tree line, he saw other Marine squads regrouping or entering into the forested hills, ACVs providing support where they could.

"Alright," Michaelson spoke over the squad radio network, Nick hearing his leader's voice clearly in his ear through the PELTOR headset while a muffled version of the real words sounded in the air around him. "We're on target so far. We need to push ahead half a klick, where we'll rendezvous with Second and Third squads, then make entry into the facility."

As he spoke, Michaelson indicated towards a satellite view map displayed on a thin computer screen on the inside of his forearm, Velcroed onto his woodland MARPAT camouflage Battle Dress Uniform.

"Move out, Marines!"

The squad raised their weapons and tactically filed through the maze of tattered trees. Once inside the forest, the sounds of battle diminished as the wall of rocks and trees deflected much of the noise. Nick could make out the chatter of distant gunfire as the Marines carefully advanced, but they had yet to encounter any enemy combatants. After about ten minutes they came to a clearing with low clumps of rock strewn about.

"The rendezvous point should be just across this clearing," Michaelson announced to the team.

The column of Marines continued creeping forward with their guns up, scanning for threats. Private Smithfield was on point, with Vasquez close behind, while Nick was near the middle of the group. Without warning, machine gun fire erupted from the trees ahead and to the left. Smithfield was torn apart as heavy rounds punched through his body, his right arm coming fully detached below the elbow and his chest plate shattering under multiple impacts. Vasquez went down as well, a bloody mess.

"Contact front!" a Marine screamed as the rest of the squad immediately hit the deck.

"Corpsman up!" came another shout.

The squad medic, a kid by the name of Lin who had been an EMT in a Chicago suburb before enlisting at the outbreak of the war, rushed towards the downed men in a hunched jog. A machine gun bullet tore through his bulky medical pack, which was sticking up off his bent back, spinning Lin to the ground and spewing bandages and packs of QuikClot combat gauze across the gray earth. Lin crawled the rest of the way to where Vasquez was lying on his back, a haunting moan emanating from the wounded soldier's lips.

"Fuck, fuck, where the fuck are they?" Michaelson asked to no one in particular, his supine form curled against the surrounding rocks.

"Fuckin' shit man!" a Marine behind Nick exclaimed.

Lying on his stomach in the pebble-strewn dirt, Nick pressed his body as close to the earth as he could physically manage. The powerful 12.7x108mm machine gun rounds were obliterating the fragile pumice boulders that the Marines were covering behind, and it was only a matter of time before the squad would be exposed to the lethal fire again.

Michaelson consulted his wrist-mounted GPS map that could show him the location of the other two squads in his platoon. Nick then heard him radio across the platoon channel.

"One is pinned down hard! Two, do you have an angle on these guys?"

"Nah man, we're gettin' fucked up out here!" came the frantic response.

"Three, where the fuck are you?"

"We're, uh, we're stuck in some fucking swamp man."

"We gotta call in a fucking air strike!" One of the First squad Marines piped up.

"Bradley, hit 'em with the forty Mike Mike," Michaelson ordered.

"Shit sir, I can't get an angle without getting my fuckin' head blown off," Corporal Bradley replied.

"Come on, we need air support," urged another Marine.

"Okay! Shut the fuck up and let me think!" snapped Michaelson.

In the background Nick heard a bellow of helpless rage from Lin, "No, no, fuck FUUUUCK!"

Nick squeezed his eyes shut, trying to block out the distant barking of machine guns, the supersonic cracks of hot lead splitting the air inches above his head, and the cursing of the Marines around him. At this moment he realized he would give anything in the world to just be back behind the counter of Little Caesars, assembling cheap pizzas from prepackaged ingredients to sell to ungrateful customers in the quiet safety of the civilized world. He'd endured strenuous mental and physical ordeals during his military training and always came out the other side unbroken, but now that it appeared the rest of his life would be measured in seconds, he was starting to crack.

A Marine next to Michaelson twisted his body around and grabbed the squad leader's wrist map and pointed to a position about a hundred yards away from their own.

"I think they're over here," the Marine said.

"Are you sure?" Michaelson asked, his voice shaky.

"I don't fucking know bro! I think so, just call it and we'll see!"

Michaelson switched to his command channel, and Nick could no longer hear the other side of the radio conversation.

"Bravo company, Second platoon, requesting immediate air support. Sending coordinates now," Michaelson called into his microphone. A brief pause separated the platoon leader's exclamations. "No, we don't have thirty seconds. We'll be dead by then!" "Yes, danger close, fucking send it!" Michaelson's panicked voice turned shrill as he screamed the last words into his radio headset.

Within seconds, the target package and firing command had been relayed to a drone operator miles away, issuing remote instructions to a General Atomics MQ-9 Reaper drone patrolling five thousand feet overhead. Nick thought he heard a distinct whistling sound, but before he could fully process the noise, his vision turned white, and he was lifted off his stomach and into the air.

Nick found himself on his back, staring up into a swirling haze of smoke and dust, his ears ringing while struggling to process any other sounds around him. A blurry figure stood over him and he could hear a hollow voice cutting through the undulating background buzz.

"Go, go, go. Get the fuck up, Delgado!"

Nick snapped to his senses and grabbed a proffered hand to pull himself up off the ground. The Marine who had helped him up was unrecognizable, his face covered in dust and soot. The other Marines were already charging into the thick brown brume, so Nick grasped his dangling rifle and began sprinting to catch up. On his way he passed by the motionless, carmine-spattered bodies of Smithfield and Vasquez.

As he waded through the devastating aftermath of the AGM-114R Hellfire II missile strike, Nick observed the twisted metal of wrecked QJZ-171 heavy machine guns. Among the debris, he noticed chunks that could only be severed body parts. Storming through the billowing smoke and licking flames, Nick felt transformed. The missile's explosion had flipped a switch inside him. The Nick Delgado who felt fear, anger, compassion, joy, sorrow, disgust; the real Nick Delgado, was locked away. The Marine, Private First Class Delgado, emerged. Sculpted by a meticulously crafted training regimen refined over decades of warfighting, forged by unrelenting adversity, The Marine was a warrior with a bias for action who would take orders and execute on them to the fullest extent that he was physically capable.

Nick moved as if in a trance as he formed up with the remnants of First and Second squads outside a metal door riveted into a blank wall of robust concrete.

"Two, sitrep," queried Michaelson.

"Four KIA sir, two wounded but they're still in the fight," the sergeant leading Second squad reported.

"We lost two," Michaelson stated. He then spoke into the radio, "Three, sitrep."

"We're still, ah, in this goddamn swamp, uh, sir."

"Fuckin' shitheads," mumbled Michaelson. Switching channels, he checked in with the company commander. "Speartip, this is Bravo Two Actual. Second platoon has reached access point Zulu, minus one squad. How copy?"

"Bravo Two, this is Speartip Oh One, solid copy. First platoon entered the compound from the south five minutes ago. They reported heavy resistance, and we haven't been able to reach them since. We suspect a total team kill. Third platoon is breaching from the west as we speak. We need you to get in there and link up with Three." Nick could hear the company commander's update over the radio.

"Can do, sir. Bravo Two out," replied Michaelson. He turned to address the twelve Marines assembled around him. "You heard the commander. Stack up by the numbers, we're going in."

A Marine next to Nick pulled out a breaching kit and began placing charges on the steel door. Nick took his place in the stack of Marines along the side of the door. He would be third into the room.

"Breaching, breaching!"

The words were punctuated by a loud pop. The two Marines on either side of the door stepped back and aimed their weapons inside, covering opposing halves of the area beyond. Meeting no resistance, the column of Marines began to file inside. Nick glided into the room in a flow state, his gun shouldered, eyes tracking for targets. He was responsible for covering one assigned sector of the room, and as he stepped past one of the breachers he raised his weapon while scanning the area before him. The space was dimly lit by a string of emergency lights running along the ceiling. The room appeared to lead to a downward staircase but was otherwise barren.

"Clear!" someone shouted.

"Moving."

The team of Marines began descending the staircase, each rifle muzzle presiding over a different angle. At the bottom of the staircase, the hallway split into a T intersection, allowing the Marines to branch either to the left or the right.

"Hold," called Michaelson.

The Marines held their positions, rifles aiming down either corridor, while Michaelson consulted his map. A couple Marines were still waiting up on the stairs, but Nick was at the landing, watching the right-side passage. He stared through his optic at a doorway about fifty feet down the hall.

"According to the layout, the hallway is supposed to go straight here…" Michaelson trailed off, "Fuckin' A man."

"Nice, so what the fuck do we do now?" questioned the Second squad team lead.

"Yea, which way do we go?" another Marine asked.

Just then, the door Nick was watching burst open. Armed figures appeared in the doorway, and it was visually clear to Nick that they were not fellow Marines. He reacted immediately, pulling the trigger of his XM5 and sending controlled bursts of 6.8mm bullets through the opening and into the armed hostiles on the other side. Three other Marines opened up with their own rifles at the same time.

The first few enemy soldiers were quickly cut down, but return fire sliced back through the clumped-up Marines, who scattered, hugging the walls and floors while dumping full magazines down the hallway. Even with his PELTOR headset selectively dampening higher decibel sound waves, the outpouring of close quarters gunfire was deafening. The booming shots blotted out the sounds of lead ricocheting off walls or shattering against armor plates, the cries of pain, and the wet slaps of bullets impacting flesh.

"Frag out!" shouted the Marine across from Nick. The young man then proceeded to hurl a fragmentation grenade down the hallway, managing to roll it through the doorway.

Nick tapped the magazine release button on his rifle with his index finger, allowing an empty magazine to clatter to the floor while he slid a fresh mag out from the front of his vest. The grenade exploded with a bang audible even over the sustained rifle fire. Razor sharp, high velocity metal fragments filled the air on the other side of the door, shredding the Chinese defenders positioned within. Nick rammed the fresh magazine up into his rifle, thumbed the bolt catch, and continued firing into the doorway.

"Ceasefire, ceasefire!" yelled Michaelson. "Delgado, Crenshaw, secure that doorway. Lin, we need medical."

Nick and the Marine who had thrown the frag grenade crept towards the door, guns up and backs sliding along the wall. As Nick approached the doorway, he had to step gingerly over the ragged bloody corpses of Chinese soldiers. The two Marines peered inside the room beyond. The room bore resemblance to a slaughterhouse, blood and guts plastered onto the walls. As Nick angled his rifle towards the far corner, his eyes caught a flicker of movement. A surviving Chinese soldier was raising a Norinco Type 95 assault rifle at him. Nick didn't hesitate. He squeezed off a long burst, walking a string of .277 Fury rounds up the man's torso and into his neck and head.

The burst put the survivor down for good.

"Clear."

More Marines moved down the hall and into the room, which contained another descending staircase. Nick could hear Lin battling desperately to save a wounded man back in the hallway. Seven Marines were now gathered in the messy room or just outside the doorway.

"Looks like we're going this way," Michaelson said, tipping his helmet towards the stairs in the corner.

Nick performed a tactical reload, stowing the partially empty magazine back in his chest rig, then began to move out with the rest of the dwindling platoon. He gave no thought to the fact that he had just taken another human being's life. Instead, he bit down on the plastic nipple of his backpack-mounted hydration system, his training reminding him that staying hydrated was vital to remaining combat effective. He was in full spectrum warrior mode.

The Marines trooped down the next set of stairs, following a straight corridor for about a hundred yards before arriving at a third stairway. Kneeling around the top of the stairs, Nick and the other Marines could hear the distant tapping of boots moving cautiously along a cement floor. Michaelson took a look at his GPS map, seeing if he could locate Third platoon. With the small mountains now above them, no GPS signal was able to get through from overhead. The ground radios, however, had much less distance to penetrate horizontally and were still functional.

"Bravo Two for Bravo Three. Bravo Two for Bravo Three," the lieutenant whispered.

The radio crackled back, "Go for Bravo Three."

The other platoon had to be relatively nearby for them to pick each other up on comms.

"Three, where are you in the compound right now?" Michaelson asked.

"Fuck if I know man. The map we got ain't worth a shit," the Third platoon soldier responded.

"Tell me about it," Michaelson quipped. "Do you see a set of ascending stairs ahead of you?"

"Yes, sir."

"Hold position."

"Holding."

The faint tapping stopped.

"Switch your scope to night mode, then tell me if you see an IR laser making a figure eight at the foot of the stairs." After making the request, Michaelson began to weave the barrel of his gun in a figure eight pattern, playing his infrared laser sight across the floor below.

"Okay yeah, I see it. That you?"

"Yep, that's us. We're coming down."

"Friendlies coming down," Bravo Three called to his platoon.

"Let's go," Michaelson said to his own platoon, leading the men down the staircase.

When they got to the bottom, they were met by about twenty Marines, many showing signs of having participated in intense gunfighting.

"Shit man, this all you got left?" the sergeant now in charge of Third platoon asked.

"Yeah, well our Third squad got fucking lost in the woods, and I can't raise them on the comm," Michaelson explained. Then he called in to the company commander, "Speartip, Bravo Two has linked up with Bravo Three inside the facility. We're not sure if we're heading the right direction. Is anyone else in here with us?"

"Negative. Fourth and Fifth platoons got skunked by a cave in. They're making their way back around to the west entrance from outside, but it will take them three zero minutes. We don't have that kind of time to wait though. We need that site secured yesterday," the commander spoke with urgency in his voice. "Tech teams are already moving into position. We're counting on you to capture the control center ASAP."

"Hard copy, sir. We'll get it done," Michaelson plainly stated.

The combined group of Marines entered and cleared another passageway, this one much wider than the last few. At the end of the hall was a large double door. Nick could hear the low thrum of electronic machinery coming from the other side. A Marine tested the door latch.

"Locked."

"This has gotta be it," hazarded Michaelson, "Set up for a breach. Be careful, we don't want to completely destroy whatever's on the other side."

The Marines positioned themselves on either side of the door, most standing with a few in low crouches ready to add firepower to the breaching elements.

"Breaching."

Fully enclosed underground, this explosive entry was

much louder than the first one the platoon had made outside the structure. Rifles tracked through the doorway, and the Marines wielding them were immediately met with gunfire pouring out from within the next room. The Marines returned fire, but several had already gone down. Nick, crouched down near the entryway, caught a brief glimpse of the space beyond, getting off a few shots before being forced to duck back behind cover.

The area ahead of them was a circular chamber about thirty yards across, with a high vaulted ceiling. Rows of computer workstations filled the center while banks of monitors lined areas along the wall. At least a dozen Chinese soldiers were holding the center of the room, firing a mix of assault rifles and machine guns from behind barricades.

"Fuck, fuck," a Marine uttered, stepping back from the opening where a continuous stream of lethal lead was zipping by.

Most of the Marines were holding positions along the walls, a few peeking around for quick potshots.

"Banger out!" a Marine shouted before blindly hurling a flashbang through the doorway.

True to its name, a piercing bang soon followed from the grenade, but the enemy fire did not abate.

"Fuck it bro I'm hittin' 'em with the forty," Bradley proclaimed, pulling out a compact Heckler & Koch HK269 40mm grenade launcher.

The Marine leaned into the doorway, a throaty pop resonating from the weapon. Right after the grenade left the launch tube, a rifle round struck the Marine in the eye socket, spraying skull fragments and brain matter onto his nearby teammates. As his body dropped to the floor in a twisted heap, a concussive blast from the other side indicated the grenade had struck its target. In the wake of the explosion, a handful of Marines slid through the door, flopping behind the cover of desks and cabinets on the other side. The enemy barrage quickly picked back up and the Marines were struggling to find openings to take action.

Nick heard the company commander come over the radio.

"Bravo Two, sit-rep. Tech teams are moving through the structure now."

Michaelson answered, "Sir, we're at the control center but we're meeting heavy resistance. We can't get through."

"Dammit, Marine. We need that room secured now, whatever it takes!"

"Yes, sir," Michaelson replied grimly.

Nick knew what was coming next. With their numbers, the Marines could make one big push through the narrow door and overwhelm the defenders, but it would be a costly assault. The first Marines through the exposed choke point would undoubtedly be slaughtered by the volume of high-powered rounds scything out from the defensive emplacement, paying the entry toll with their lives to get the Marines behind them through the breach.

Following the hellfire strike outside, where the austere Marine programming had assumed control within Nick's mind, his fear of death had departed along with his other soft human emotions. It still pained him greatly, however, to see his Marine battle brothers meeting their end.

While these thoughts played out through Nick's mind, his warrior's senses detected a change in the cadence of gunfire emanating from within the room ahead. The deep reports of outgoing 7.62mm and 12.7mm rounds were overtaken by the higher pitched clacking of 6.8mm shots. Picking up on the cessation of hostile fire, Marines flooded into the room, Nick storming the breach with them.

It took Nick a second to register what he was seeing across the round control center. A group of humanoid figures, covered from head to toe in thick black mud and grime, were approaching the rear of the Chinese barricade from the far end of the room. The mud men, looking like golems that had risen up out of the earth, had weapons trained on the now silent defensive emplacement. Only the whites of their eyes and teeth indicated that they were, in fact, human.

"Friendlies, friendlies, hold fire!" one of the mud men shouted.

"Identify yourselves!" Michaelson screamed back.

"Fuck, dude, it's me, Rogers. With Third squad."

"Son of a bitch," a Marine beside Nick exclaimed.

"We have some non-combatants here," the muddy Rogers said, waving the barrel of his rifle towards a cluster of unarmed men and women cowering on the floor between rows of hardware.

"Get them zipped and let's set up a perimeter," Michaelson ordered the assembled Marines. Then into his radio he called in to the commander. "This is Bravo Two, Matchstick is secure, I repeat, Matchstick is secure. Send in the eggheads."

"Alright," the leader of Second squad addressed Rogers, "so what's your fuckin' story?"

"Well fuck bro, like I was sayin' to Mikey. We walked right into that fuckin' swamp, and like I don't know we just kept pushin' forward cuz Oorah an shit. But it just keeps gettin' deeper and deeper, and before ya know it we're swimming in the shit, and I mean literally in the shit. At that point our fuckin' comms were all mucked up and we had to ditch half our gear just to keep from fuckin' drowning," Rogers took a deep breath before continuing. "When we finally got out, we were way the fuck off course, so we followed the map to X-ray. Fuck bro, when we went in, we found all of First platoon. Fuckin' wasted, every last one of 'em. That was fucked up man. Looked like they took a ton of the fuckin' bastards down with 'em though. Anyway, we decided then that we needed to kill every last one of those Chi-com fucks, so we start sprinting through this fuckin' maze. We heard what sounded like a fuckin' fourth of July celebration going on so we followed our ears, and here we are."

By then, the technical team had entered the room and were plugging into computer consoles and workstations.

"Motherfucker," Michaelson mused.

"Motherfucker," another Marine echoed.

"We lost a lot of good Marines taking this piss-forsaken

shithole," Michaelson spoke with an edge of frustration in his voice. "It sure as fuck better be worth it."

CHAPTER 47

Low Earth Orbit
December 10, 2034
1455 Hours JST

Strapped into the boarding capsule and docked within one of the launch bays of a Perseid carrier, Kenneth felt like a passenger on an elaborate rollercoaster ride. As the carrier accelerated and decelerated, the forces acted on him inside the capsule. Compared to the crew of the carrier though, he had much less insight into what was taking place outside the walls of the ship. This was nothing new. He'd been transported via all manner of conveyance vehicles on sea, air, land, and space. He had even grabbed a couple hours of sleep during the long approach at constant velocity, but the unpredictable bursts of violent acceleration made that impossible now.

Securely buckled in next to him was Captain Damien Brown. The only other survivor of the station assault months ago, Damien had become Kenneth's right hand man on the Space Force Security Operations team. Though their capsule was pressurized and held breathable air, the two men were already bundled up in protective space suits in anticipation of an EVA walk, only leaving their faces exposed to the chilly recycled compartment atmosphere. They had both docked with and boarded satellites before as part of various training exercises, but never when the stakes were so high.

"You boys awake back there?" the pilot of the carrier they were riding in asked.

"Yee-up, and bored as hell," Brown responded.

"We're drifting into the final orbit now, we should be ready to deploy in about ten minutes."

"Copy that, we ain't goin' anywhere."

Kenneth closed his eyes and listened in on the squad channel.

"Approaching the ball, stay wide."

"I'm picking something up, wait one."

"Okay that looks like debris, confirming…"

"Vampire, vampire!"

"Venus Five is hit!"

"We're in a field of sleeper drones! Spread out and get ordnance on any unverified signatures."

Kenneth twisted in his seat to look at Brown.

"Shit man, Robin and Markowitz were in Venus Five," Brown stated sullenly.

The voice of one of the co-pilots cut in over the shipboard channel, "There's a laser locked onto us, it's melting through our hull."

"Executing longitudinal roll," the pilot tersely informed her passengers.

Kenneth suddenly felt himself being pressed against the left side of the capsule. He felt Brown's shoulder digging into his right side. The carrier had gone into a spin to distribute the energy of the laser evenly across the fuselage, preventing it from inflicting any serious damage. While it saved the ship from harm, Kenneth and Brown were now being twirled around like t-shirts in a laundry cycle.

"The laser stopped," reported the co-pilot.

"One of the Gammas tagged the firing platform," said the third crew member who was overseeing the drone squad.

With that, the pilot fired the compressed gas thrusters to counteract the spin, bringing the ship back to comfortable stability once more.

"We're in range to launch the boarding capsule."

"Copy, launching capsule."

Kenneth felt a mild vibration running up through his seat

as the capsule detached from the carrier. He grasped the plain joystick in front of him, preparing to assume motive control. As the capsule left the carrier bay, the view through the resilient cockpit glass in front of him flipped from the dark metallic interior of the ship, to the majestic curving horizon of the Earth juxtaposed over the infinite black sheet of space.

"Green team is free, maneuvering to the Baseball," Kenneth announced to the local fleet.

He knew that generals at the highest echelon of command were most likely listening in right now, raptly monitoring the status of the operation. Kenneth daintily worked the controls of the small vessel, sidling up alongside the satellite.

"Green team is up to bat. Preparing for EVA," Kenneth broadcast. Turning to Brown, he told the operator, "You're up chief."

Wordlessly, Brown unbuckled himself from his seat, drifting slightly inside the small compartment. He then sealed his helmet and ran through his pre-spacewalk checklist, double and triple checking over all of his gear. Secured across his chest on a broad patch of Velcro and backed up with a tether running to the harness around his waist was the computer expropriation kit prepared by a team of highly talented cybersecurity and engineering experts. Within the kit were physical tools to gain access to the satellite's local computer interface, as well as hacking components that could be inserted locally to override the satellite's remote command network. Each component inside the kit was attached with a piece of coiling plastic wire to prevent them from floating away, and all were uniquely shaped for easy ergonomic use by an individual wearing EVA gloves.

Once the hack was completed, Brown would be able to feed targeting solutions and firing commands directly into the computer that controlled the eight hypersonic glide missiles mounted with high-yield nuclear warheads mounted on the satellite. While neither man was aware of the exact targets, they knew the strike would be hitting key Chinese cities. The list most likely included Beijing, Shanghai, Guangzhou, and

Shenzhen, placing upwards of one hundred million people in the blast zones.

Kenneth ran hands and eyes over Brown's equipment, running all the same checks himself to provide redundancy. With Brown's helmet now sealed shut, Kenneth spoke to him over the radio.

"You're good to go."

Brown pulled himself over to an airlock chamber barely large enough to fit a single person in full EVA kit. Sealing the interior door, he activated the airlock and the chamber began to depressurize. While he waited for the process to complete, Brown secured himself to the tether mounted to the wall of the vessel within the airlock. Once the chamber was fully depressurized, the exterior hatch slid open, and Brown slipped out into the ocean of emptiness.

Kenneth had parked their miniature ship close enough that Brown was able to reach out and latch on to a side panel on the satellite with a magnetic clamp without having to trigger the compressed gas thrusters in his Simplified Aid For EVA Rescue, or SAFER, backpack. Brown worked his way along the satellite, clamping and unclamping as he went, until he found the access panel exactly where the mission briefing had indicated it would be.

"Green Two is ready to swing," Brown called into his communication microphone.

From his angle in the cockpit, Kenneth could only see Brown's dangling legs while the operator went to work on the satellite access panel. Kenneth tried to relax as his brother-in-arms individually performed the momentous task that the success of this entire elaborate operation hinged on. He listened intently to the comms chatter going back and forth.

"Access panel is removed. I can see the computer interface," Brown reported.

"Standby," came the weighty voice of General Ironwood. "PACOM confirms that all Matchsticks have been secured. Green Two you are clear to execute."

"Copy," Brown replied hollowly.

Kenneth sat motionless, his body on edge while Brown facilitated the hack that would send nuclear hellfire raining down upon mainland China.

"HT device is in the blue port," Brown said, corroborating what the command staff back on Shepard station and a team of engineers down on Earth could all see through Brown's live suit camera feed.

"Okay, override is confirmed," stated the head engineer. "Next, insert the target package feeder into the yellow port directly to the right of the blue port."

"It's in."

"Okay...looks like targeting solutions are set. General?"

"We are go for Home Run. I repeat, go for Home Run," Ironwood pronounced.

"Copy, General. Alright Green Two, now pull back the manual release and the launch sequence will engage."

Kenneth held his breath. It seemed that Brown was hesitating.

"Green Two?" the engineer queried.

Brown opened up a private channel to Kenneth.

"I...I can't do it."

"What do you mean? Is the hardware jammed?"

"No...I, I just can't pull that lever, sir," Brown sounded as if he were on the verge of tears. "All those people down there. I can't do this to them. I can't be responsible for this."

Kenneth cogitated on this for a moment. He understood exactly where Brown was coming from. The men had both taken plenty of lives in battle, but this was tantamount to murder. Their fight was with the dictatorial Chinese Communist Party, not the people forced to live under the oppressive regime. Sure, the deaths of millions could bring an end to a war that had the ultimate potential to kill billions, but Kenneth knew he could never live with himself if he were the executioner snuffing out all those innocent lives, and he knew Brown must feel the same way.

Ironwood's brash voice interrupted Kenneth's reverie.

"Green Two, what's going on up there? Are you alright? Pull the damned lever already!"

"Sir, I'm sorry. I can't."

"What the hell do you mean you can't? Do you know how many good men and women gave their lives today to put you in this position? The position to end the war, right here, right now!" Ironwood's surprise was morphing into fury. "I am giving you a direct order, soldier. Pull. That. Lever."

Brown had nothing to say in response. He remained frozen in inaction. Kenneth knew that this was killing his comrade. Brown was as loyal as they came. Kenneth had personally seen the man willing to lay down his life to carry out his duty as a defender of the republic. Defying his orders and failing to achieve a mission objective was anathema to the career soldier. And yet, he had finally found his limit. A line he could not cross. A line Kenneth would not cross either.

A new voice came in over the radio.

"General what the hell is going on up there? Why haven't the missiles launched yet?"

"Mr. President, sir, our operator is unwilling to carry out his orders to initiate the launch."

"Are you kidding me? We're this close to winning this war, and it's all going to shit because some pussy is now a conscientious objector? Why can't we just push the command remotely?"

"Sir, in the computer's fallback state, the missiles can only be released by disengaging the security lock manually," an engineer chimed in.

"For Christ's sake," the President let out an exasperated groan. "Have someone else get out there and do it."

"Green One, get out there and complete the mission," Ironwood ordered.

Kenneth's conflicted mind was churning. He had sworn an oath of loyalty to his country, and Kenneth valued his honor over his own life. But Kenneth placed his loyalty to his team, to his family, and to God above all else, absolutely. Not only was Brown a member of his team, but as a battle brother he had shed blood with, Brown was also, for all intents and purposes, family. Furthermore, Kenneth knew that when his time finally came, he could never face the Lord with the blood of millions of unjudged men, women, and children on his hands.

"Green One!"

"Sir," Kenneth spoke coldly into his microphone. "Green Two said he is unable to pull the lever. We're aborting the mission."

An angry cacophony filled his ears though the headset, but he ignored them and switched over to the private channel with Brown.

"Damien, come on back."

CHAPTER 48

John F. Kennedy Conference Room, a.k.a. "The Situation Room," Washington D.C.
December 10, 2034
1520 Hours JST (0620 EST)

The President of the United States of America was livid. Beyond livid. The veins on his neck were taut against the skin, his face shading a ruddy red.

"Who are these men? Get another team up there! I don't care if one of those fighter jock pilots has to bail out and do the damn thing themselves. Make this happen now!" the President rambled on, flailing for a solution.

One of his more level headed cabinet members took over with a more reasonable line of questioning.

"How much time do we have left to act?"

"In thirty minutes the orbital path will pass out of the high-confidence hit zone," an engineer on the other side of the country responded. "Another ten and we're looking at a severely diminished targeting capacity. Beyond that, we lose all strike capability."

Voices clamored over each other as the assembled collection of self-important men and women vied to make their opinions heard. The Secretary of State, a thin, serious woman with closely cropped gray hair, put her hand on the President's shoulder and spoke into his ear.

"Silence!" commanded the President.

The frantic moil quickly subsided.

"Stacy, you were saying?"

The Secretary of State cleared her throat then began.

"I believe we can still use the current situation to our advantage and possibly even accomplish our overall objective. Look, we've got China by the balls right now, and they know it. While they've lost the ability to control this satellite, they can still pick up and decode the targeting outputs. They know exactly where we're aiming those nukes right now, and there's not a damned thing they can do about it. As far as they know, our operator is standing by, reading and willing to pull the trigger as soon as we tell him to. For the next thirty minutes, we have the ultimate bargaining chip."

"So what you're saying," sussed out the President, "is that we push for an immediate unconditional surrender, under threat of nuclear destruction."

"They'll never agree to that," interjected a balding general with a wall of service ribbons holding position over a rotund beer gut.

"Even if they do, what's to stop them from going back on their word as soon as the strike window closes?" questioned another.

"Now that," the Secretary of State resumed, "is why we must be very specific with our terms. We will give them a comprehensive list of satellites; the Space Force has a list of known and suspected offensive and defensive space based weapons platforms; and demand that they deorbit every last one of those satellites immediately. If they don't, we fire on them, and wipe eight of their most important cities from the map. In addition, we must make it clear as soon as we begin the discussion that any continued hostile actions against our force guarding the satellite will be interpreted as a refusal of our terms and grounds for us to fire."

"I don't know. I don't see them playing along with that game," Ironwood chimed in over a live video feed.

"I don't think they'd have a choice," the President opined. "We have Beijing in our sights, and they know they'd never recover from a blow like this. Besides, they lack the capability to hit us back with anything near this level of strength," he paused before adding coldly, "Right, General?"

"That is correct, sir. Our defensive measures will stop 99.5% of any munitions in flight against us," Ironwood assured.

"And General," the Secretary of State began interrogatively, addressing Ironwood, "we could detect right away any adjustments in their satellite trajectories that would result in irreversible rapid orbital decay, correct?"

"That is also correct, ma'am."

"And once those satellites are all out of play," the President jumped in, "We would have the standing to force a permanent surrender."

"Precisely," the Secretary of State said with a wolfish grin.

"Well, what are we waiting for? Get Xi on the line."

CHAPTER 49

Low Earth Orbit
December 10, 2034
1536 Hours JST

"They're crossing the horizon again," one of Maria's pilots informed her.

"I see. Looks like they'll be in range to fire any minute now," Maria replied.

Maria wasn't sure what the current status of the mission was or what those screwball door-kickers were doing with the satellite right now. All she knew was that no nuclear missiles had been fired yet and that her orders were to continue to defend the satellite and the team that had docked with it. As she braced for the enemy force to resume their attack, she acknowledged that the only way such a defense would end was with the destruction of her own ship and all of the units in her command. Maria only hoped that sometime in the next ten minutes, the astronauts performing the satellite hack could move past whatever barrier was preventing them from completing their mission so that the sacrifice of her pilots would not be in vain.

"Uhh, are you seeing this? It looks like they're decelerating again," the other pilot said, unsure of himself.

Why would they be doing that? Maria wondered. It wouldn't make sense if they were preparing to fire. Maybe they were making a small correction to their flight path, but again that seemed unlikely given that their computers should have had the trajectory locked in perfectly from the start. Perhaps they misread the threat Maria and her squadrons posed?

"Yeah, they're definitely decelerating, hard," another pilot called out.

"They're retreating, they're turning around!" the first pilot proclaimed, cautiously optimistic.

Maria spoke into her microphone to address her confused pilots.

"I don't know what their game is, but stay frosty."

CHAPTER 50

Alan Shepard Space Station, Geostationary Orbit
December 17, 2034
1100 Hours CST

The atmosphere around the station had been one of giddy celebration in the wake of the previous week's operation. It was as if Christmas had come a little early for the beleaguered station personnel. Rob had been studiously consuming news updates by the minute in an attempt to grasp what was happening down on Earth. Amazingly, China had agreed to effectively disarm themselves in space, giving the United States near total dominance. India and Russia still possessed some orbital assets, but the United States now held a monopoly on space-based missile defense architecture.

The war was over. None of the other members of the BRIC alliance were willing to face down NATO without China as their backbone. The exact fate of China remained to be determined. The United States had agreed to allow the current regime to remain in power, and even to retain most of their conventional armed forces. Vulnerable to nuclear strikes as they were, however, their military capabilities were essentially neutered when it came to full scale conflict. Rob suspected that China would continue in her role as a powerhouse industrial producer. The world simply could not get by without it.

For himself, Rob had decided that he had had enough of the extraterrestrial life. With the war at an end, he didn't feel that his services were a matter of existential necessity anymore, and he planned on asking for leave to return to his home in the

Upper Peninsula of Michigan as soon as transportation could be arranged. He wasn't sure what he would do when he got there, but his experiences over the past few years had given him a confidence that left him hungry to pursue whatever opportunities life might throw at him.

Above all else though, Rob felt a primal need to reconnect with nature. He yearned for the vast crystal blue waters of Lake Superior, and pined to be among the ocean of conifers and hardwoods. Space certainly held a hypnotic beauty that he would not soon forget, but he had been born a child of the Earth, and mother nature was calling him home.

CHAPTER 51

City of Xinzhou, Shanxi, China
December 20, 2034
1832 Hours China Standard Time

Qing was awed by the results of his treachery. He was no fool. Despite the claims being made by the Party that they were acting in the interest of global peace and for the benefit of all mankind, he recognized that their hand had been forced. He had also cross verified the timeline of events with the orbital path of the militarized Huanjing satellite he had revealed to the CIA. Through one simple act of espionage, he had single-handedly put in motion a series of events that brought the Chinese Communist Party to its knees. Hai-Ping would be proud. His parents would be proud. And now the only dark thoughts to pierce the cloud of satisfied euphoria he was feeling were of his parents' safety.

  The CIA handler had offered him an escape from China, knowing that their utilization of his intelligence would likely burn Qing as an asset. They could not make the same offer for his parents, however. Qing already doubted the capabilities of the CIA to keep him safe from the epidemic reach of the Party. He knew that by fleeing, or attempting to flee, he would be proclaiming his guilt to the government, thereby ineluctably condemning his parents to a miserable end.

  Thus, he concluded that his best course of action was to simply continue living his life as normal - to raise no undue suspicion. Perhaps the overgrown Chinese intelligence arm would be too busy dealing with the fallout of their shift in global status to chase down the source of the leak. His office had undergone a lockdown and subsequent investigation in the wake of the December 10th announcement, but as of yet he had not been pulled from his bed in the middle of the night with a bag over his head by Ministry of State Security goons.

Strolling down the sidewalk on his way home from the market, his paranoia was unrelenting. Qing cringed as a man in a dark trench coat stepped out in front of him. The man stared at him for a second, then squeezed by. It was just cold out, that's why he was wearing the thick coat. Another man stood, leaning against a doorway smoking a cigarette, his eyes scanning the crowd. No, he was just reading the newsreel across the street.

Qing jumped when he felt a hand on his shoulder.

"Mr. Li, please come with me."

Qing turned around to face a smiling gentleman wearing a smart gray pinstriped suit and a black bowler cap. Despite the man's friendly demeanor, his words carried a menacing undertone that chilled Qing. Qing complied without protest. If this was what he suspected, there was no use resisting.

The man led Qing to a nearby sedan. A pristine 2030 model. The man opened the rear door and ushered Qing into the back seat, then slid in after him. The front seat was empty. At some unseen signal from the man in the suit, the car began to move, maneuvering itself with the use of high fidelity external sensors and a powerful onboard computer.

The windows were not blacked out, no blindfold was placed around Qing's eyes, and his hands and feet remained unbound. The eerie civility belied the inimical nature of the business. The two men sat in mute tranquility as their robotic chauffeur ferried them to their destination. After ten minutes of passing by nondescript city blocks and faceless crowds, the car entered into an industrial district and pulled into a poorly lit garage.

The man unbuckled his seatbelt, exited the vehicle, then walked around to open Qing's door, motioning for him to step out as well. The pair walked through a rusty door into a small room where a pair of beefy men in well-tailored suits that fit their broad frames tightly were seated along an uncomfortable looking bench, staring at their cellphones. The men glanced up as Qing and his escort entered, each giving a curt nod to the man beside Qing before turning their attention back to their phones.

Qing's chaperone led him down a musty staircase into a damp unfinished basement. Most of the space lay in shadowy darkness. Qing could sense that the room was quite large and that there were other objects present, but underneath a bright light he could not make out what the shadows hid only a few feet away from him. A set of strong hands grasped each of Qing's arms, placing him under firm arrest.

The suited man who had rendered Qing to this cryptic chamber, who Qing now assumed must be an MSS agent, stepped forward, then called a name that Qing could not make out. Another bright light clicked on at the other end of the basement, revealing two figures about ten feet away. The figures were fully naked, their hands shackled above their heads by chains running down from the ceiling. A female and male. His mother and his father.

Qing's gut twisted, and he felt as if he might vomit.

"Qing!" his mother screamed, "Qing! Qing! Oh, Qing."

She was crying, but she did not sound sad. Instead, it appeared that they were tears of…joy?

"Qing!" his father called out. "Think nothing of our suffering! You have made us more proud than you can possibly imagine. We gladly go to join your sister now that her requited soul may rest."

"Enough!" the MSS man shouted, covering the distance to Qing's parents in a few long strides and landing an open handed smack on the side of Qing's father's face loud enough to echo off the enclosed walls of the basement.

"Now," continued the MSS agent, a look of pure disdain contorting his face, "for a traitor like you, I have a special show lined up. Only the lowliest of life forms could have possibly come together to breed and create scum such as yourself, so we shall begin by ensuring this blight on civilization is forever removed from the world."

With that, the man drew a long, ugly blade that had been concealed within his suit jacket. Qing's parents remained stoic, undaunted by the cruel instrument. Without further ceremony, the man walked over to Qing's mother and made a long, shallow cut along her belly, evoking a sharp cry of pain. Qing felt a cry of his own well up within him, but he locked eyes with his father and the two maintained their impassive stares.

The torture continued in this manner for what felt like hours. The sadistic MSS man making shallow cuts all across Qing's mother's body, the lifeblood slowly draining out of her until she hung pale and limp. At this sight, Qing's father began to weep, but he managed to call out to Qing before being silenced by the MSS butcher.

"She died happy, Qing, as will I. Our family will soon be reunited in bliss!"

Next, the MSS man moved on to Qing's father, repeating the same agonizing process. Qing looked on in a stupor, forcing his mind to drift towards memories of his family, especially of his sister. At some point the men holding Qing's arms released him, and he dropped to his knees, unmoving. When the MSS man finally finished with Qing's father, he approached Qing.

He reached out towards one of the other men standing beside Qing, who placed a small black pistol into their leader's hand.

"You," the MSS agent spat, "are lower than a dog. It is hardly worth my effort to spend more time punishing a mixed egg. Your life has less value than the single bullet that will end it."

"Fuck you and eighteen generations of your ancestors. Your line is that of the Mogwai!" Qing retorted fiercely. "I face death gladly knowing that I have acquitted myself nobly and honored my family. Kill me, you son of swine!"

Indignant rage flashed across the MSS man's face, his mouth turning down into a bitter snarl. He did not reply. He simply raised his pistol to Qing's forehead.

"Mother, father, Hai-Ping, I am on my way," Qing whispered.

The suited man's finger curled around the trigger of the QSZ-92A pistol, the pressure building until it overcame the friction of the sear, which slipped out of its notch. This released the hammer, driving the firing pin into the primer of the chambered 9x19mm Parabellum round. The rapid expansion of gasses within the brass cartridge expelled the copper-encased lead bullet from the barrel of the pistol at over one thousand feet per second. The bullet traveled the inches to Qing's forehead in less than a millisecond.

The bullet pierced the thin skin of Qing's forehead and bored through his skull. Microseconds after the foreign metal object began displacing brain matter, Qing's body registered the infliction of a fatal wound. Microscopic glands in his brain secreted the chemical dimethyltryptamine, inducing his mind into a rapturous hallucinatory state. As the chemical dispersed throughout the blood-brain barrier, the molecules started binding to various serotonin receptors.

Qing's visual processing became overwhelmed by a soft white light and his conscious perception of time slowed down by orders of magnitude. Nanoseconds felt like hours. Hai-Ping appeared before Qing, a loving smile on her face, filling Qing with joy. His parents appeared behind her, the trio simply silently smiling at him. Hai-Ping held out her hand, and Qing took it. His perspective zoomed out, his mind departing from his physical body.

Qing became an omniscient observer to a tapestry of human experience playing out before him like the most vivid and sensually engrossing film ever created. He bore witness to ancient civilizations rising and falling, feeling immense exaltation as his soul basked in the glory of achievement and renaissance, colligated with intense grief and despair as war, famine, pestilence, murder, and genocide all had their turn.

Some of these events Qing identified from his broad

knowledge of history, others were completely novel. Days passed for Qing in this phantasmal state, stunning truths were revealed and unsolved mysteries of the past were answered for him. He watched as dynastic families traded control over Chinese lands, saw Ghengis Khan ravage the Mongol steppes, and puzzled through displays of advanced technologies that seemed wholly anachronistic. As time progressed, the episodes became more recognizable and the modern world he knew from his own life started to take shape.

Eventually Qing's own life took center stage, flashing before his eyes in bromidic fashion. He watched the man in the suit raising the pistol to his own head, saw the shot fired, and watched himself collapse onto the floor. The Earth continued to turn, billions of lives carried on, and as he had seen time and again on this fantastic journey, geopolitical power vacuums were filled. Humans expanded their reach into space while improving their mastery over the physical universe down to the quantum level.

Structures on the moon took form and massive fleets traversed the solar system. Then suddenly the Earth lit up with flashes of intense light that gave way to thick umbral clouds obscuring the sapphire sphere. Qing was working to comprehend this latest development when Hai-Ping appeared again, this time at his side.

"Brother, let us go."

Qing followed Hai-Ping towards a field of brightening light, Narashimono sounds wrapping him in a sonorous embrace. In that moment, Qing felt a sense of sublime satisfaction.

Qing's body fell back onto the cold, hard basement floor, all detectable neurological activity in his brain having ceased.

ACKNOWLEDGEMENT

Anne Stadnik - Test Audience

Rick Waldo - Moral Support

Lee Weinstein - Jarhead Consult

Made in the USA
Coppell, TX
05 December 2022

87850043R00142

ABOUT THE AUTHOR

Matt Charles

Matt lives in Interlochen, Michigan, with his wife, dog, and cat. He holds a degree in Physics with a concentration in Astrophysics from Stanford University and has always possessed a deep interest in space flight and exploration. He spends many of his weekends in the Upper Peninsula hiking, climbing, and paddling.

If you want to share your thoughts on the book, drop him a line at mattcharlesbooks@gmail.com